I0522370

A HEART'S

Promise

Corrissa James

Copyright © 2014 Corrissa James

All rights reserved.

This book or any portion thereof may not be reproduced or used in any manner whatsoever without the express written permission of the publisher, except for the use of brief quotations in a book review.

ISBN: 0692384626

ISBN-13: 978-0692384626

Inkwell International

Laurel, NE 68745

www.inkwellinternational.com

A HEART'S

Promise

Chapter One

The people of Bender, Nebraska, knew Trish Cassidy to be an easygoing woman who playfully teased nearly everyone in town, so when she moved into the apartments run by Bruce Garrison, a hot-headed and greedy man who thought the world owed him something, the local tongues wagged about how long Trish would be able to tolerate Bruce as a landlord. When Trish and Bruce started dating, it nearly caused a riot among the gossips. Now, sitting on the makeshift bench provided for wait staff on breaks and rubbing the tears from her eyes, Trish knew the latest drama would send the rumor mill flying once again. She couldn't believe what a fool she'd been, believing Bruce's proclamations that she made him a better person—that he loved her, truly and deeply, despite his increasing demonstrations of jealousy. And now he'd assaulted her boss, a man who had been nothing but kind to her and who clearly only had eyes for the tall brunette sitting at the table with him. Bruce wanted Trish to quit her job. His antics today would undoubtedly result in her losing it. *And it's a damn good job!*

Tilting her face to the bright blue sky, she let the early Sunday afternoon sun dry the salty tear streaks on her cheeks. The new sheriff had come to haul Bruce to jail, explaining he'd be locked up until the judge arrived tomorrow morning. Trish hadn't missed his implied meaning: Get her stuff packed and get out from under his thumb before tomorrow morning. Easier said than done, of course. With only a few thousand people in the city, Bender did not have much in the way of rental housing, and not many people would be willing to deal with Bruce showing up on their doorstep once he found out where Trish moved to. So here she sat, outside the service entrance of the hotel where she worked, letting the sun warm her face while she ignored the simple truth: She would have to leave Bender.

Trish reached up and pulled her strawberry-blond hair over her shoulder to braid it, her fingers quickly working through the long tresses. It was a habit she'd picked up since her parents' death. Sitting in the hospital after the accident, waiting for news about her parents, she'd braided and unbraided her hair hundreds of times. Now it helped her think, her brain working through the problem as her fingers worked through her hair.

She didn't want to leave Bender, but with no job and no place to stay, she didn't think she had much of a choice. If only she had found work on a farm, she wouldn't be having this problem now. Unfortunately not many farmers were willing to hire female managers, not even the corporations that were snatching up the farms at an alarming rate. Trish had spent the small savings her parents had left her for her degree in agri-business—a sound investment everyone had said at the time considering her goal of managing and eventually owning her own ranch—but now here she was, about to lose her waitressing job. The few hundred dollars left in her bank account would not sustain her through the end of the month. Her fingers reached the end of the braid, paused, then pulled it all out. She combed through her hair and started braiding once again.

"Excuse me."

The deep voice startled her, and Trish focused on the tall man standing a few feet in front of her. How had someone so tall, so imposing, sneaked up on her without her noticing? She suppressed a shudder and dropped her hands to her lap, affecting the polite pose her mother had taught her was appropriate for ladies. "Yes?"

"I'm looking for Jake Monroe."

"Just through there. Follow the hallway until the end. The front desk will know where he's at."

"Thanks." The man reached for the door, then glanced back at her. "You okay, miss?"

"Oh, no need to be dusting off your white hat." She shooed him toward the door.

"Well, you certainly don't look like a damsel in distress, it's just..."

Trish watched him, curious about what he would say.

He shoved his hands in the pockets of his faded jeans and pursed his lips. "It's just, you look like you need a friend right about now."

She crossed her arms in mock indignity. "I'm pretty sure eavesdropping on ladies' thoughts will get you kicked out of the White Hat Club."

He shrugged. "Their meetings are pretty boring."

"I know, right? It's all 'I saved this damsel, I saved that kitten'—we've heard it all before. Where's the excitement?"

"In the Black Hat Club, naturally."

Trish raised an eyebrow. "Oh, you're one of those."

"Gotta be true to who I am." He reached out a hand. "Dalton, by the way."

"Nice to meet you, Dalton By The Way. I'm Trish On The Bench."

His handshake was firm but relaxed. Still, Trish could feel an intense power pulsing just beneath the surface.

"So, Trish On The Bench, can you help a fellow out?" Dalton sat down next to her. "I'm kinda overdue for my White Hat badge this month."

"Fine." She rolled her eyes in an exaggerated fashion. "But don't say I didn't warn you. This is pretty boring stuff."

Dalton cleared his throat and turned to focus all his attention on her. He reminded her of a little boy trying to prove what a grown-up he was. Trish couldn't help but smile.

"Oh a smile! One point for me."

Trish applauded. "Nicely done. Now try this one on for size: My jerk of a boyfriend—make that ex-boyfriend—just punched out my boss, so I am pretty sure I'm gonna lose my job."

Dalton laughed a deep, throaty laugh that Trish felt rumble through her core.

She rolled her eyes. "Great. At least I can still entertain a handsome stranger."

He placed his large tanned hand over hers on the bench. "Jake's not going to fire you for what your ex does."

"It's not the first time he's caused trouble." Trish pulled her hand out from under his, pretending to check her fingernails as she wiped away invisible dirt. In reality she'd been disturbed by the surprising heat his hand had generated in her, sending shocking warmth reeling up her arm.

"So why have you stayed with him?" His caramel-brown eyes studied her face.

She shrugged. "Nobody else needs me, I guess."

He frowned.

"Plus, he owns my apartment complex." She nudged his shoulder with hers. "Not smart to piss off both the landlord and the boss in one day, but that's how I roll."

Trish glanced up when the service door opened. Jake stepped outside and looked around until he spotted them on the bench. "Hey, Dalton. Sorry man. It's been a crazy day."

"Yeah, I was just hearing about it." He didn't take his eyes from Trish.

Jake clapped him on the shoulder, then motioned for Dalton to follow him inside. "Oh, hey Trish, go talk to Mrs. Jackson in the front office."

Trish gave Dalton a "told you" look as Jake led him inside. Only after he disappeared through the door did she realize she'd been holding her breath.

Chapter Two

Dalton James followed Jake into the manager's tiny office, but he couldn't stop himself from glancing over his shoulder to see if the blond woman had followed them inside. He was disappointed to see the door at the end of the hallway remained closed. His mood soured when he realized he was more focused on her than his current situation. Chasing skirts would have to be put on the back burner, at least until he could get the ranch rebuilt. Besides, taking advantage of women in distress was not his style. He didn't have time for the emotions, the clinginess, the walking on eggshells because of a woman's past hurts. All people dealt with pain. He'd certainly had his own fair share of it, so playing the victim did not sit well with him.

Yet Trish didn't seem to be playing the victim card at all, which intrigued him—so much so that it was taking every ounce of restraint not to go back outside so he could...

"Earth to Dalton."

Dalton's eyes snapped back to his friend. "Oh, sorry. Got distracted for a minute there."

"No problem. I've got my own distractions today."

Dalton flashed him a knowing grin. "So I heard. Did you at least get a few punches in?"

Jake's brow furrowed in confusion before he glanced at the door, understanding washing over him. "She pretty upset?"

"I think more about her job than the boyfriend, who sounds like a real winner." Dalton eyed his friend for a moment, debating his next question, not certain he wanted to know the answer. "So I'm guessing the boyfriend has a jealousy problem. Anything to it?"

The cloud of black anger that passed over his friend's face caused Dalton to inhale sharply. He was clutching at the arms of his chair and moved his hands to his knees instead, berating himself for his own feelings related to Trish. He'd just met the woman, for crying out loud.

"Bruce Garrison is so low he makes the bottom of the barrel look saintly. Why any woman would choose to be with that scum is beyond me."

Dalton forced a grin. "So you didn't get any punches in."

"I was more worried about Mel."

"This character took on two of you at once?"

Jake drummed his fingers on his desk and scowled at Dalton. "Melanie."

Dalton stared at his friend for a moment, confused. When he suddenly understood, he threw his head back and laughed so loudly his voice echoed off the office walls. When he looked back at Jake, the scowl on his friend's face had deepened, which made Dalton laugh even harder.

"Yeah, yeah. Hardy har har."

Dalton wiped at the tears in his eyes. "The mighty Jake Monroe, finally felled by a woman?" He noted Jake's frown. "You're kidding. She didn't appreciate you standing up for her?"

"She's not my concern. But you didn't come here to discuss my problems, did you." Jake pretended to arrange the papers on his desk, letting his anger mask his pain.

Dalton shrugged. If that was how he wanted to play it, who was he to say otherwise?

When Jake finally looked up, he said, "Your message this morning said it was urgent."

"Did I say urgent?" Dalton winced.

"Some things never change."

"Actually, I wanted to get some names from you. I, um, need some trustworthy guys to help with rebuilding the ranch." He waited for that nugget of information to sink in.

It didn't take long for Jake to smile. "So you're going to make an offer on the land I showed you?"

"Already did. Signed the papers on Monday. Had everything moved in by Wednesday."

Jake whistled. "It's a good investment, but I didn't think you'd be able to convince Miranda of that, not so quickly, at least."

Dalton snorted. "I think 'convince' might be too strong of a word. Besides, I used my own money."

"Well, congratulations. And welcome to the neighborhood. But sorry to tell you, I hired all the trustworthy workers—and don't you even think about stealing them from me."

Dalton threw his hands up in mock surrender.

"I don't suppose you'd consider taking on Mr. Garrison, just to get him out of my hair?"

Now it was Dalton's turn to scowl. "If that's the best Bender has to offer, I am better off doing it all myself."

They spoke for a few more minutes, mostly about the best suppliers of construction materials in the area, before Jake was interrupted by a call from the front desk. Dalton signaled to him that they'd talk later as he slipped out the door. He hadn't gotten the information he needed, so he wasn't sure why his step was so light as he pushed open the heavy door that led outside. Surely it couldn't be because of the blond he'd met earlier. Yet when his eyes adjusted to the afternoon sun and he saw that the bench was empty, he knew the disappointment he felt had nothing to do with his thwarted plans to rebuild his ranch.

Chapter Three

Trisha frowned. *Go talk to Mrs. Jackson in the front office.* The words sounded so ominous, so final, but not at all unexpected. She braided her hair once more, wrapped a band around the bottom to keep it from unraveling, then steeled herself to deal with Mrs. Jackson, who was likely preparing the paperwork to fire her. Trish's frown deepened as she walked down the hallway. She actually liked her waitressing job, even though she'd always said it was just temporary until she could find some work on a farm. This job had enabled her to meet a lot of people who came in to see the new hotel, and she'd made sure to give them the best service she could. More importantly, she made connections that she knew she could cultivate. Now she was going to lose it all.

Including the chance to see the handsome Dalton.

Her step faltered when she heard Dalton's laugh coming from Jake's office. She stopped in front of the door, shifting closer to hear what made him laugh with such abandon, telling herself she was merely curious and that her actions had nothing to do with her racing heart. Surely that was because she was about to face Mrs. Jackson.

Trish shook her head before continuing down the hall. "Don't get distracted now, girlfriend," she mumbled under her breath. After all, her distraction list was already full up for the day.

Mrs. Jackson sat behind a small desk in her office. The desk looked even smaller with Mrs. Jackson's girth piled up in the chair behind it. Her 1960s reading glasses sat on the tip of her nose so she could look up at people when they needed to talk to her. Most people avoided talking to Mrs. Jackson because they were afraid of her. She didn't let anyone get away with anything. Ever. But Trish knew the older woman was just darn good at her job and took it seriously, drawing a very well-defined line between her professional and personal life, ensuring that the two never met.

"Mr. Monroe has asked me to talk to you." Mrs. Jackson scowled at Trish. "You are not to live in Mr. Garrison's complex any longer."

Trish opened her mouth to argue the point, but Mrs. Jackson cut her off by clearing her throat loudly and purposefully.

"He has offered you a room to stay in—at no cost, despite my strong objections—until you can arrange other accommodations." Mrs. Jackson eyed Trish. "Which I expect to be sooner rather than later."

Trish started to protest, to say she couldn't accept such an offer, but Mrs. Jackson seemed to know what Trish was thinking and raised a long, slim eyebrow at the girl. Trish finally just nodded.

Mrs. Jackson read from a piece of paper on her desk. "No maid service will be provided, so you will clean up after yourself. No long distance calls. No charging anything to your room." She slid the paper to Trish. "Sign and date."

"And my job?" Trish didn't look up while signing the agreement, afraid the room was being offered to soften the blow.

Mrs. Jackson harrumphed loudly. "Anything stopping you from working?"

Trish shook her head.

"Then carry on. Business as usual." She handed Trish a key card but didn't let go when Trish tried to take it. "Young lady, I hope you know what a gift this is. I trust you will use it wisely."

"I will, Mrs. Jackson, I promise."

It took Trish less than an hour to box up her personal items. She looked around the apartment. She was leaving the furniture, kitchenware, and knick-knacks, all of which she'd paid for. But space was limited, and she wasn't going to return once Bruce was released in the morning. Everything would have to be replaced when she found another place to live. It would be more expenses that she couldn't afford, but she wouldn't have to worry about Bruce and his stupid antics anymore.

She was walking through the hotel lobby, an overnight bag slung over her shoulder, when Mrs. Jackson came waddling out of the office. Trish had never seen her move so fast, which didn't bode well.

"Ms. Cassidy. Maybe I didn't make myself clear." She pointed to a large box sitting just inside the lobby entrance. "I don't know what it is and I don't care, but it smells and it's your responsibility."

The box seemed to vibrate as Trish neared it. On the outside was a note scrawled in dark letters: "For Trish On The Bench—someone who needs you." She lifted the lid slightly. A black nose wedged itself between the box and the lid, pushing the lid back farther until it fell away to reveal a black puppy with a large pink belly. It yipped once, then sat staring up at her, its tongue lolling to the side. Giggling, she scooped the puppy into her arms, where it snuggled into her neck and promptly fell asleep. Trish's heart melted, and she wanted to squeeze the puppy in a tight hug.

No, she couldn't get attached.

Trish sighed, knowing what she had to do and suddenly angry that she'd been put in this position. It was going to be hard enough finding a place that would rent to her thanks to the Bruce issue; finding a place that accepted pets—and a puppy, no less— would be impossible.

She knocked on the office door and stuck her head inside. "Mrs. Jackson, do you happen to know the man who dropped this, uh, package off?"

"No, I do not." Her voice was clipped, and she didn't look up from her paperwork.

"Excuse me, I meant his name—or maybe an address?"

Mrs. Jackson looked over her glasses to Trish without lifting her head. "You know very well, Ms. Cassidy, that we do not give out personal information on guests, employees, or vendors—or friends of Mr. Monroe."

"Yes, I know, but—"

"No buts, Ms. Cassidy. I will not break the rules."

Trish pushed open the door and stepped into the office, the puppy still nestled in her arms, asleep. "Yes, well, as I am sure you know, any employee who receives an unsolicited gift is to bring said gift to the front office. That's what the employee handbook states, correct?"

"Indeed." Mrs. Jackson eyed the puppy, a scowl forming on her lips.

"So, where shall I put him?" Trish nodded at the puppy.

Mrs. Jackson's scowl deepened, and her face turned a dusty rose that had nothing to do with her makeup. She scribbled something on a piece of paper, never taking her eyes off the dog, then held the slip up to Trish. "Don't make me regret this."

"No, ma'am. I won't." She snatched the paper from the woman and hurried out of the office before Mrs. Jackson changed her mind. Once back in her truck, she placed the puppy on the seat next to her, but he scrambled onto her lap and snuggled in, back to sleep in no time. On the paper Mrs. Jackson had written: *Dalton James, old Schmidt ranch, 2 miles north of Hwy. 20 on River Road.* It wasn't an area she was familiar with.

"Hope you're up for an adventure, pups."

The puppy sighed in his sleep.

"See? Now that is what Sunday afternoons are all about."

She stroked his soft fur before starting up the truck and heading north of town.

Chapter Four

Dalton had been heading to the ranch when he saw the sign along the highway advertising dogs for sale. On a whim, he headed down the gravel road until he came upon a large, well-kept farm with several kennels lined up along the edge of the property. Twenty minutes later he was heading back to town to find Trish and show her the black lab puppy. Jake had already left and wasn't answering his cell, and the large woman behind the desk could not be charmed into giving up one iota of information about Trish, although her frowned deepened considerably when Dalton asked about Bruce Garrison. Frustrated, he put the puppy in a large box and left it in the lobby.

Now, as he drove back to the ranch, he was beating himself up for his stupid idea. The dog was for him, to help him keep an eye on the ranch. And, if he was completely honest with himself, to keep him company. He didn't mind the quiet during the day, but he'd never liked the stillness at night, especially after he started living with his father, a bitter man who often took out his frustrations on his children after the sun set. Dalton had been fifteen at the time. He had tried to remain stoic in the face of his mother's illness, but she'd sent him away to live with a man he'd never met—a man who already had a family of his own.

Dalton never saw his mother again.

He pulled into the lane leading to the two-story farmhouse, his mood blackening with each passing moment. Today was not turning out at all like he'd planned. And now he'd left a puppy in a box for a woman he'd just met—a woman with no place to live. He barely stopped the truck before throwing open the door and jumping out, slamming the door with such a ferocity that Cyrus, his Friesian stallion, looked up from his meal of dry hay. The powerful and proud horse was intimidating to most—standing seventeen hands tall—which was one reason why Dalton had offered nearly twice what he was worth to get him—an investment he had not regretted once. Cyrus trotted to the fence as Dalton climbed over. The fact the horse was not bothered by Dalton's black mood spoke volumes to the man and actually tempered the edge on his anger.

Moments later, Dalton was on Cyrus's back, leading him through the six-foot wide path he'd hacked through the overgrown riding area in order to gain access to the open pasture. Clearing the area was one reason he'd wanted information from Jake. The path continued for maybe a thousand yards beyond the riding area before opening up into grasslands where Cyrus was able to run, but it had taken Dalton an entire day to cut through the weeds and scrub. He needed workers, and he needed them now.

When he gave Cyrus free rein, the horse took off at a powerful gallop, as if sensing his rider's need for the run as well. Dalton was forced to focus all his efforts to stay on the horse's back as the animal moved through the field, around sandhills, and past clusters of cottonwood, ash, and cedar trees, never slowing once. He felt his frustration melt away and was able to enjoy the ride, reveling in the power of the animal. Ten minutes later, when they reached the end of the property line surrounding Dalton's twelve hundred acres, he slowed Cyrus and let him walk the two miles back to the house, stopping at the creek that wove through the southern part of the property to drink his fill. By the time they returned to the riding area, Dalton was focused once again on the ranch. He decided to make a list of materials he needed to get the bunkhouse up to par so that if he could find workers, they had a place to stay. Once he was able to offer housing, maybe he could find some willing ranch hands to bring the long-ignored property back to its glory days. He would deal with Trish and the puppy fiasco tomorrow.

But when Cyrus stomped his front leg, Dalton's attention was diverted elsewhere. He turned to see a truck driving down the lane, the driver's blond hair sending a shock of excitement through his body.

Chapter Five

Trish eyed Dalton, not sure she'd heard him correctly. "Wait, did you just—"

"Stay here."

So she wasn't imagining things, though her imagination was running rampant with images of staying with Dalton and all that could entail. To cover the warmth she felt creeping up her neck, she leaned against her truck and feigned indignity. "Well, that's mighty forward of you, sir."

Dalton held his hands up and took a step back. "Oh, no, that's not what I meant."

"What? Why not?" Trish planted her fists on her hips. "Am I not good enough for you?" She burst into laughter before she got the last word out, unable to maintain the charade. The puppy that had been sitting at her feet stood up to bark at Dalton. "You tell him, pups." She scooped up the puppy and let him lick her face. Dalton hadn't refused to take the dog back, but he hadn't agreed either. She appreciated his willingness to offer an alternative, but it still didn't solve her long-term needs.

"Look, you seem like a nice girl, and clearly you need a helping hand."

Those few words were enough to bring Trish's anger roaring to life. After her parents' accident, many in the community had reached out to her, trying to help. But Trish soon learned that their help came at a price. Either they would pass judgment on her, telling her how to use what they offered, or they expected something in return. "I don't take handouts, Mr. James." Her voice was scathing and cold.

"Don't call me that. Ever." The coldness in his voice matched her own. They stared at each other for a moment, their furies escalating in unison.

The puppy's howling made Trish turn away first. He was still in her arms, but struggling to free himself as he watched a large black horse trot up to them in the ring. It stopped a few feet from the fence they stood next to and snorted. Trish put the puppy in her truck and closed the door, then walked back to where the horse was standing. She held out her closed hand to the horse, as if offering a snack. The horse nosed her hand, but when she opened it, it was empty. He snorted once again, but Trish was already rubbing its long nose and it calmed instantly.

"Clearly you have experience with horses." Dalton's voice was more relaxed, with a hint of surprise.

"Parents had a ranch." Her voice was clipped as she was still trying to shake off her anger. The surprise in his voice didn't help. Trish sighed. *Yet another person who thought women's work was reserved for the kitchen—and maybe the vegetable garden.*

"Had?"

"They're dead."

The horse stepped closer, nuzzling her hand, demanding a treat.

"He doesn't do that—let people touch him."

"So now you're saying I'm not human?" Her attempt to lighten the mood fell flat, and both she and Dalton shifted uncomfortably.

Inside, Trish groaned. Why did she feel so unnerved by this man? And why wasn't she jumping at the offer for a place to stay? One look at him in his black t-shirt, which hugged his nicely molded arm and chest muscles, and she knew that her hesitation stemmed from her attraction to him. She didn't want to jump from one ill-formed intimacy to another, only to find herself homeless yet again in a few weeks. Still, the images of a shirtless Dalton fluttered through her mind as if trying to convince her that those few weeks might be well worth the ultimate inconvenience.

Dalton took off his cowboy hat and wiped his forehead, then looked down at Trish, his dark eyes sizing her up. "Look, there's a whole bunkhouse you can have to yourself." When she glanced at the large house, he said, "I know how people like to talk. The bunkhouse isn't pretty and needs some work, but it'll stop the wagging tongues. Well, give them pause at least. You and the dog are welcome to it."

"In exchange for...?" She was mortified by how suggestive the question seemed in her mind, but it didn't seem to have any effect on him.

Dalton shrugged. When Trish still didn't accept, he looked toward the horse. A smile spread across his face that nearly took Trish's breath away, and she almost didn't hear his next words. "For helping me get this place back to a working horse ranch."

A new kind of excitement seared through Trish as she scanned the area. The old two-story house still seemed as grandiose as when it was first built, although it desperately needed a loving touch, maybe some new paint or, better yet, some new siding. The rest of the spread was in more dire need of help. The weeds in the fields were easily waist high, and she saw Russian knapweed in the mix. They'd have to eradicate that before allowing horses into the fields. The horse ring and stable already had fundamental repairs, but many areas would be problems if more than one horse were on the land. She looked back at Dalton, giving him a look that told him exactly what she thought of his project. She walked to the bunkhouse, which was in a truly sorry state. When she opened the door, it fell off one of the hinges. The inside needed some serious attention too—and fast.

"I'll give you room and board—for you and the puppy—plus $300 a week," Dalton said from behind her, startling her. "Sundays off."

She walked back outside for another look around, making him wait in silence. The ranch had promise, and she could already envision it as a premier equestrian facility. It would be a lot of hard work, but she would be stupid not to accept his offer.

Trish turned back to him. "$500 a week and I get one of the horses once we get going—my choice."

Chapter Six

Dalton stood with his arms crossed and a deep frown on his face. She was crazy. Hiring her had been an impulsive move that he couldn't really afford, especially at the rate she demanded, but now watching her toss everything out the front door of the bunkhouse made him realize that her charm might be a mask for her insanity.

"I'm serious, woman!"

Trish moved to stand in the doorway. Dust already covered her face and hair, and she coughed a few times while staring at him. Her coughing caused the puppy, which was sleeping on the bunkhouse porch, to wake up and immediately start barking at Dalton once again. She hushed him, then threw what looked like the remnants of a mattress onto the debris pile she'd started.

Dalton gritted his teeth before trying once again. "We can't make this place livable today. Just stay at the hotel until we can."

"I'll get a lot more done if I don't have to drive back and forth to town, not to mention the savings in gas money." She threw a three-legged wooden chair on the pile.

"For what I'm paying you, gas isn't going to be a problem." He mumbled his retort, not thinking she could hear him. The sour look she gave him proved otherwise.

"Listen, Mr. James—"

He reached her in two strides, grabbing her arm roughly. "I asked you never call me that," he hissed.

She turned her cool blue eyes up to him. "Why not?"

Her question startled him. She had not asked out of fear or anger but out of curiosity—despite what he knew must be a painful grip on her arm. He let go but did not move away from her.

"It's okay. You don't have to tell me." Her voice was soothing, as if she were speaking to a child who had just broken his favorite toy. "We all have secrets." She stepped back, still looking at him. She paused a moment to smile, then turned around to resume her cleaning.

Dalton ran a hand through his hair and exhaled slowly. His body remained tense, loathe to let go of the anger. It festered just below the surface, seeking a release. He knew he should walk away, leave her to finish cleaning the bunkhouse out herself, but he wanted to stay near her, listen to her grunts as she heaved the junk outside and study her face to see where new dust patches appeared. What he really wanted to was run his thumb across her cheek to brush off the errant dust. He scowled. Agreeing— no, asking!—her to stay here had been a mistake, but he had absolutely no intention of revoking the invitation now.

She stepped back into the doorway and chucked an armful onto the debris pile. "Besides, going to town wouldn't be the smartest thing right about now." She wiped the sweat from her brow, leaving dirt streaks in the wake. "Mind you, I don't think he'd be that stupid, but it's probably best Bruce not know where I'm staying, right?"

Her smile felt like a laser tearing through his chest as Dalton realized that she was, in fact, afraid of her ex, although she seemed to be trying to hide it through her playfulness. And if she was afraid, it meant that he had likely hurt her in some way. Remembering how tightly he'd just gripped her arm and her pacifying response, Dalton bellowed in frustration. He stormed into the bunkhouse, pushing past a startled-looking Trish, and started grabbing leftover furniture and trash, hurling it through the doorway with a viciousness that caused Trish to step back, the shock registering on her face.

He knew it was the wrong way to act, especially around her, given her all-too-recent history, but he couldn't stop himself. His fury at Bruce erupted and had no other outlet. If the man were here, Dalton would strangle him until he begged forgiveness. Hell, he might not even stop then. But Bruce wasn't here, so Dalton took out his anger through cleaning, which enabled him to ignore the voice in the back of his mind pointing out that he wasn't as mad at Bruce as he was at himself. Thanks to his actions, Trish likely thought that he was just as bad or even worse than Bruce. No matter what he did, he had to prove to her that he was not that man—he was not a man who let his anger hurt those around him. He was not his father.

Unfortunately, he was afraid that he was exactly that kind of man.

Chapter Seven

An hour later, Trish was scrubbing every last inch of the room while Dalton repaired several holes in the walls and reattached the door. She had recognized his attack on the bunkhouse as a way to work out whatever demons were plaguing him, so she had not interfered—except to salvage the single bed frame, a red enamel coffee pot, and the old wood stove before he trashed those as well. It had required most of the last hour for him to tire himself enough to calm down, although she suspected his anger was still lurking just beneath the surface.

She also knew that his anger wasn't the same kind of anger Bruce had let loose on her. Her ex felt sorry for himself, as if everyone in the world had it better than he did. By putting her down a notch or two by calling her a bad waitress or a bad girlfriend, he could convince himself that he wasn't the lowest rung on the ladder. Dalton's anger wasn't focused on pushing her down, but rather on covering something up. Some pain from his past maybe?

Watching him work through the bunkhouse, seeing his muscles working and the sweat glistening on his arms as he hefted boxes of junk out the door, she knew he was turning that anger inward. Yes, Dalton James certainly had his secrets, and she could live with that, although the overpowering urge to hold him might be the death of her.

She had never been so excited about cleaning as when he finally got everything out of the bunkhouse and she started sweeping out as much of the dust and dirt as she could. Finally she could focus on something other than Dalton, and the clouds of dust inside meant he was forced to wait outside. Unfortunately, her reprieve was short lived. When she started scrubbing the room down, he started working on the little fixes he could do with his tools at hand, such as rehanging the front door. She did have to admit that having a door on the bunkhouse would only be proper.

It was well after dinner time when they stepped back to examine their work.

"A fresh coat of paint, a mattress for the bed frame, and maybe I can scare up a table and chair and this will do very nicely."

Dalton eyed her, not hiding his look of doubt. "You clearly haven't taken a look at the bathroom yet."

She stepped farther into the bunkhouse, but Dalton moved to stand in front of her, blocking the way.

"No, really, I think we've done enough for today. I don't want you quitting on the first day."

Trish laughed. "There's nothing in there that's gonna scare me." A look of shame washed over his face as she pushed past him. When she stepped back and closed the door, she said, "So maybe I spoke too soon. Probably should have looked in there before I made a mess of myself." She brushed at her clothes. The plume of dust and dirt she stirred up made her cough.

Dalton shook his head, which caused more dust to fly into the air. "Not good. C'mon—and bring the pup."

Trish scooped up the sleeping puppy, which was now a dusty gray. He yawned and looked at her, then fell right back asleep in her arms. "Such a hard worker," she whispered, snuggling him close as she followed Dalton.

It was still light outside. The summer sun didn't completely set until 9:00 or even later in Nebraska, and Trish figured they still had an hour or so before dusk set in. Her stomach suddenly growled loudly, protesting that it had been ignored too long.

"Yeah, yeah, I know," Dalton grumbled.

She shrugged. "You did say room and board."

After he saddled Cyrus, Dalton went to the main house, then returned a moment later, carrying two small bags that he shoved into the saddlebags before pulling himself up. He held out a hand for Trish, and she handed him the puppy before swinging up onto the saddle behind him.

Sitting so close to Dalton, she inhaled the mixture of his scent—an earthy smell that was likely from his shampoo or aftershave mingled with the sweat of hard work. It was a manly scent that she could easily get lost in for days.

Dalton walked Cyrus away from the stable and down a barely graveled path that soon disappeared into knee-high grasses and weeds. Trish could feel Cyrus pulling and testing Dalton. The horse wanted to take the lead and do what came natural to horses, but Dalton was keeping a tight rein on him. Too bad. Trish would've liked to see what the horse could do.

The path they followed dipped into a small alcove, then led up a hill. At the top, Dalton stopped to appreciate the view.

"Twelve hundred acres, plus another three hundred or so to the west for the family's cattle."

Trish could understand the pride in his voice. She looked out on gently rolling hills dotted with trees. The land seemed to have been forgotten, thriving without the interference of human meddling. The beauty of the land was matched by the intensity of the enormous soft blue sky that extended above them. She felt as if she really could reach up and touch the heavens. She sighed. "You can just leave me to sleep out here tonight. Every night, in fact. I would never leave."

She felt Dalton's muscles tense before he nudged Cyrus to move on. She was glad that he couldn't see the embarrassment burning in her face. Her declaration, especially about never leaving, made her sound borderline stalkerish. Never mind that she had felt so at ease around him that her naturally flirtatious nature had been in fine form. And now they were riding together— after he basically told her to move in with him. He probably worried that she was reading into the situation, and her comment only played into that fear. She would have to convince him that she saw their relationship as strictly platonic. An employee–employer situation.

As they continued along the path, she noticed a stand of mulberry trees whose fruit hung heavy on the branches. "Can we head that way for just a second?" When she pointed at the trees, her stomach growled even louder.

Dalton laughed as he turned Cyrus toward the trees. Trish gathered several handfuls of mulberries and put them into the small bag Dalton produced from the saddle, stopping to pop more than a few of the deep purple berries into her mouth. But Cyrus was growing impatient, so they moved on to the next hill, where they took no time to appreciate the beauty. Cyrus wouldn't stand for it. The horse was growing increasingly antsy, and Dalton gave him a bit more of free rein. Trish soon realized why.

They descended the hillside into a line of cottonwoods that snaked back and forth, stretching out before them. Cottonwoods meant one thing: water. Sure enough, Cyrus led them right to a creek flowing through the middle of the trees. The horse tried to stop as soon as they came to the water's edge, but Dalton turned him and nudged him a bit farther to the north until they came to a small pool.

Trish slid off the horse and made her way to the edge of the pool, setting the pup down. He sniffed the water, drank from it, then pressed his entire face underwater, followed by his chubby belly. "Wait for me, fella!" As if on cue, the puppy pulled himself back out of the water, shook off as best he could, then looked up at Trish and yipped three times.

"I'll watch him. You go first." Dalton handed her a towel and a bar of soap.

"You trying to tell me something, boss?"

Trish was smart enough not to laugh when she saw his cheeks flush a light pink. He went to sit under a tree, turning so his back was to the pond as he held out some jerky to lure the puppy to join him.

Moving downstream a bit, Trish found some larger rocks still dappled in the fading sunlight despite the canopy of trees above. She knew she was filthy, covered in dirt and dust, but she hesitated before undressing. Normally she wouldn't be caught dead wearing only her underwear in front of someone she had just met—and her boss to boot—especially when she suspected he was already misinterpreting her actions. But based on what she'd seen in the bathroom, she wasn't sure when she'd have a chance to shower.

Glancing once more behind her to make sure she was prudently out of Dalton's line of sight, she removed her t-shirt and capris and shook off as much dirt and dust as she could before rinsing them in the cool water. She wrung them out several times, then placed them on the still-warm rocks. They wouldn't dry completely, but she could handle a little dampness.

The pool turned out to be deeper than she anticipated, with the water coming up to just under her breasts. She dunked her head under the water, rinsing all the dirt from her hair. The soap lathered up into a fresh lilac scent—not something she would associate with Dalton, but she'd only known him one day. It felt like she'd known him so much longer. Did the soap belong to his wife? He hadn't mentioned a wife, but he had mentioned that the cattle belonged to the family. If he were married, it would make sense that he put her in the bunkhouse instead of the giant main house. Trish knew she definitely needed to keep a boundary between them.

When she felt at least somewhat human once again, she exited the water, dried off as best she could, then used the towel to dry her long hair. She shrugged into her damp clothes.

"All yours."

When Dalton glanced up at her, she heard his sharp intake of breath and saw his eyes darken to pools of deep brown. She held the towel out to him, but his eyes were focused on her, traveling the length of her body before returning to her face. Normally Trish would be offended by such an obvious act, but instead she felt a wave of satisfaction knowing that she could tempt him—although she immediately tamped that wave back down, deep into herself. *Boundaries.*

He snatched the towel from her and made his way to the pond while Trish sat next to the tree. She was somewhat put off when the puppy followed Dalton to the water, sitting at the water's edge to watch him bathe, but she forgot all about his preference for Dalton when she turned to the food laid out on the blanket. She took a bite of a biscuit and realized it was a good thing he had his looks because his culinary skills left something to be desired. She decided to abandon the baked goods for the cheese and apple he'd packed as well, making a mental note of all the things she would need to get from the store.

She took a bite of the apple and felt the hairs on the back of her neck ripple to attention. She glanced over her shoulder without thinking. Seeing Dalton's broad bare chest caused her to nearly choke. Luckily, he was soaping up his black hair, wet strands falling over his ears and face. His hair was a bit longer than accepted by traditional standards in the small town, but Trish thought it suited him well. Her new boss was a handsome man, no doubt about it, but he was her boss, so watching him bathe probably wouldn't be the best choice she'd ever made. She turned back to the food, but the hair on the back of her neck was still sending her warning signs.

The dog growled, then yipped. When his yips turned into barks, accompanied by Cyrus's whinnies and foot stomps, both Trish and Dalton scrambled to the water's edge. The pup was facing off with a juvenile black rat snake.

"Take the dog," Trish said to Dalton as she snatched up a large stick from the creekside. She slid it under the snake and let it coil around this new "intruder." She lifted the stick and, holding it at arm's length, carried it to a tree, where the snake was all too happy to take refuge.

When she returned, Dalton was standing barely waist high in the water, holding on to the dog that was struggling to get away and go play with his new friend. She held out her hands for the dog, but Dalton was focused on where she had freed the snake, the scowl darkening his features even more than normal. "I hate snakes. It's not coming back, right?"

Trish almost laughed. The snake was probably more terrified of them and wouldn't strike unless attacked, so there was really no reason to be afraid of it. Still, she saw the seriousness etched into Dalton's frown and bit back her sarcastic retort, shaking her head instead.

Dalton stepped out of the water, moving to stand next to her without taking his eyes off the tree. "We should go. Just in case."

"Um, Dalton?"

He finally glanced down at her. "Yeah?"

"Can you put some clothes on?"

Chapter Eight

Dalton didn't speak during the ride home, but Trish didn't seem to mind. He was aware of every shift she made from her perch behind him, of the hand lightly holding on to his side to keep her from accidentally slipping off. The other arm held the sleeping puppy, which he could feel pressed against his back. He fought the urge to twist in the saddle and take the animal from her so she could circle both arms around him, but she was probably still smirking over his reaction to the snake. He couldn't stop the shudder that moved through his body when he thought about the intruder, which only increased his frustration.

His skinny dipping had not helped the situation. Such a stupid decision, he realized now, but he always swam naked. He was just always alone when he did. He was furious at himself. Never in all his life had he made so many foolish mistakes in one day. What was it about Trish that had him tripping over his own feet?

No, that wasn't fair. It wasn't her. It was all him. He was acting on impulses instead of being the logical, calculating man that his father had trained him to be. His hands tightened into fists, inadvertently pulling on the reins. Cyrus shook his head, pulling back against Dalton and letting him know that he was not pleased with this development. Dalton breathed deeply, forcing himself to relax. He didn't want to be his father and deep down he knew he wasn't—he couldn't be, could he?—but he could still use the lessons his father had taught him.

His lips spread into a smug smile. He used his father's own teachings to best the older man, buying the coveted grazing lands out from under him with the money his mother had left him. It was a sweet revenge. Of course, it would have been even better had the man lived to see it. His son had manipulated the cattle company that Randall James had spent his entire life building. But Dalton also knew that his gloating—and there undoubtedly would have been gloating—would have only spurred Randall to retaliate. Now, with Randall gone, Dalton had only Miranda to deal with.

Luckily, they saw more eye to eye, having both survived the elder James's life lessons.

He wondered what Miranda would think of Trish. Miranda would undoubtedly congratulate him for hiring a woman. Frustrated by the lack of women in positions of power in rural businesses, she was on a crusade to change that. She talked a good game, but Dalton knew she had a jealous streak a mile wide. For now, it would be better to keep Trish all to himself.

Cyrus topped the last hill and, sensing that his stable and food were near, trotted the rest of the way to the barn. Dalton fought the urge to take another quick tour of the property. The sun had set, so they wouldn't see much of anything, but he didn't want to lose the warmth that was behind him. He knew it was selfish, not to mention dangerous for Cyrus, but his impulsiveness was demanding to be heeded.

Trish slid off the horse, making the decision for him, and he followed suit.

"So, bright and early tomorrow, boss?"

She was still holding the puppy, which was making his best effort to get down. Finally, she dropped him on the other side of the fence. She didn't look back toward Dalton. In fact, she looked anywhere but at him.

"I'll have the coffee ready." His attempt at a light-hearted answer sounded strained.

"Night, then."

He watched her walk toward the bunkhouse, stopping at her truck to grab something out of the back. She didn't look back at him. Scowling, he walked Cyrus into the stable. He removed the horse's saddle and rubbed him down, desperately trying not to think about the woman in the next building. Avoiding her wasn't going to work and he knew it. He was attracted to her. So why hadn't he just charmed her into bed instead of hiring her? Now he was her employer, which meant she was off limits. His father's laughter echoed in his ears. This was a situation that Randall would have found endlessly entertaining. That realization sent Dalton's anger spiraling, making it even harder to control. Even from his grave his father could humiliate him.

Dalton finished with Cyrus and headed back to the house, determined to prove that he could put his attraction to Trish aside and treat her just like any other ranch hand. Halfway to the house, he glanced toward the bunkhouse and nearly tripped on his own feet. The light in the main room was on, giving Dalton a clear view of the inhabitant. He stopped to watch her moving back and forth in the room, every once in a while bending down out of view. Suddenly she picked up the puppy and hugged him to her chest. He watched the smile spreading across her face and heard her laughter when the puppy squirmed in her embrace.

It was the laughter that was his undoing, that caused the desire to surge so powerfully inside him that he stumbled as he moved toward the bunkhouse. He wanted to tickle her with kisses, hear her husky laughter and know it was only for him—even if it meant a lifetime of humiliation from his father's voice.

Dalton lurched to a halt, inhaling sharply. Trish had put the puppy down and was now stretching her arms and yawning, a slight arch in her back that managed to send his desire so out of control that it was painful. She pulled her shirt over her head, revealing the light pink bra that he knew matched her panties. He'd tried to give her all the privacy she needed at the creek, but he was still a man after all. The few glances of her long blond hair cascading over her shoulders and down her back as she moved into the water had required every ounce of willpower to prevent him from joining her.

Now, watching her undress, his willpower was completely depleted. He would have this woman, would tease her body until her desire was as overpowering as his, then would bring her over the edge with him. And he would do so tonight, right now, employer–employee rules be damned.

Trish looked out the window. A second later, she stormed out onto the porch, not bothering to cover herself.

"Who's there?"

Her voice was hard but not hard enough to hide a sliver of fear. Dalton swore under his breath. He waved. "Sorry, just me."

"Dalton?" The immediate softening in her voice made him moan, which he hid by coughing. "You scared the bejesus out of me. I thought Bruce—well, you know."

Hearing her say Bruce's name was like a splash of ice water in his face. "Just finishing up with Cyrus. 'Night."

He stormed to the house, determined to get inside and put more distance between them, along with a couple of solid walls. Why was it that everything he did reminded her of Bruce? He swore if he ever got a hold of that lowlife, he would not walk away unscathed—if he walked away at all. For now, Dalton would have to make do with a cold shower, something he expected to be doing a lot of in the coming weeks. He would not take advantage of his authority over Trish, he would not be another Bruce in her life.

And first thing in the morning he would get privacy curtains for every damn window in the bunkhouse. A vision of Trish stretching popped into his head. Maybe he would get two or three sets of curtains, just to be safe.

Chapter Nine

Trish was awake before dawn the next morning, but not because she was anxious to get to work. Rolling up the blankets and sleeping bag, she stretched her neck and back. Sleeping on the floor had been rough, and she knew she'd feel it in her back all day. Finding a mattress for the bed frame got moved to the top of her to-do list. She wouldn't be much of a worker if she couldn't sleep.

"Like a mattress would solve that problem," she mumbled as she put on a thin, long-sleeved cotton shirt and her work jeans. A vision of Dalton came unbidden to her mind, his tall frame walking out of the creek, the water sliding down taut muscles bronzed under the sun until it reached the dark hair just under his navel. And then continued lower. She shook her head, trying to dispel the vision, but instead, Dalton was standing on the shore, close enough that she could feel the heat from his body, could reach out and touch him if she wanted to. And she had wanted to. Dalton was the kind of man women swooned over, and Trish was no exception.

Except he was her boss—a boss who had given her a once-in-a-lifetime opportunity that she was not going to throw away. She was determined to pour her blood, sweat, and tears into this ranch and make it what it deserved to be. Once she proved herself to Dalton, she'd demand a job as the ranch manager. Enduring some sleepless nights while her brain regaled her with never-ending visions of Dalton's strong jaw, caramel eyes, and soft lips was a small price to pay—as long as those visions were kept to the night-time hours, when she was alone. During the day, it was all work, only a professional relationship with her boss. No problem at all.

So why was she just standing in the middle of the room?

"Because, you ninny, you're afraid you might molest the poor guy the next time you see him."

The ride back from the creek had been the most nerve-wracking fifteen minutes of her life, sitting so close to him and wanting to lean against his back, snake her hands around his waist, kiss the back of his neck. And when she caught him standing outside the bunkhouse, why had she reacted with suspicion? If only she'd let him come to her, she would have been able to taste those lips—and so much more...

The knock on the door and subsequent yips from the puppy brought her out of her reverie. She threw open the door, and the puppy ran through it to jump on Dalton's feet.

"Traitor," Trish said.

"Excuse me?"

She shook her head and could smell the lilac soap on him, but somehow it only made him even manlier in his black shirt, dark jeans, and cowboy boots.

"I didn't wake you, did I?"

"Nope, I was just busy talking to myself."

He smiled, and Trish muffled a groan. How was she going to be able to work side by side with him without throwing herself at him? *Because he is your boss*, she reminded herself in her best Mrs. Jackson imitation.

"I brought you some paint." He pointed to three cans and some rollers sitting outside her door. "Leftovers from the house, so I can't promise the colors will be to your liking."

"Oh no, sir. That wasn't part of our agreement." Trish crossed her arms. "I distinctly remember saying $500 a week, a pick of the horses, and paint to my liking. This just won't do."

He chuckled and nodded at the main house. "There's some coffee in the kitchen. Just use the side door."

"Oh my God, I could kiss you, you sweet man." She pushed past him as he shuffled uncomfortably at the door to the bunkhouse. She tightened her jaw. It was good to know that the thought of kissing her made him uncomfortable. This boss-employee relationship would be easier than she thought.

"I left a list of things you can work on while I'm gone."

Trish whipped around. *Gone?*

"Running to town." He was halfway to his truck. "I'll be back this afternoon." He waved as he pulled out of the drive.

The puppy sat down next to Trish's feet and whined.

"I hear ya, pups."

The side door opened onto a mudroom, with a small bathroom and a washer and dryer to the right, what originally would have been a servant's bedroom to the left, and the kitchen straight ahead. The puppy went into the bedroom and whined.

"Oh, knock it off, Traitor—and yes, that name seems to suit you well, doesn't it?" Trish noticed the hastily made bed and clothes thrown over a chair in the corner. "Great, now I know how to sneak into his bed in the middle of the night." She scooped up the puppy and headed to the kitchen. "Thanks a lot for that little tidbit of knowledge, you little whiner. Now I will never sleep."

After pouring a cup of coffee, Trish searched the kitchen for something for breakfast. She found the rock-hard biscuits, a small hunk of cheese, half a gallon of milk, and some leftover steak in the fridge and wondered if this was what Dalton meant by "board." She broke apart one of the biscuits and cut up a small hunk of steak for the puppy, then laughed when he cleaned off the pieces of biscuit with his tongue but refused to eat them.

"Yeah, we'd better fix that, huh? Or we're both going to starve."

Searching through the cupboards provided better results. She rolled up her sleeves and whipped up a new batch of biscuits, then decided to make a second batch while the first one was baking. She also made some sourdough bread dough and set it on the stove to rise the rest of the day. After cleaning up her mess and wiping down the counters, she sat down to eat a warm biscuit and drink a second cup of coffee. She finally noticed the list Dalton had left her and bristled as she read it. Her "jobs" for today consisted of cleaning the kitchen, weeding the garden behind the house, and painting the bunkhouse.

She frowned. "Looks like you're not the only traitor, pups." Why had she expected anything different? "At least we can mark the kitchen off the list."

After washing out her coffee cup, Trish and the puppy headed to the back of the house to scope out the garden. She burst out laughing at the large square of knee-high weeds, but when she moved closer, she could see tomato and cucumber plants desperately trying not to be suffocated by the invading grass. Her laughter was replaced with anger. The garden would be producing well if it had been taken care of. She stormed off to the garage, where she found work gloves, a shovel, some smaller spades, buckets, and a wheelbarrow. When Dalton returned, they were definitely going to have a talk about what exactly constituted the "board" part of room and board.

"You found all of this in that overgrown garden?"

Trish felt the pride surge in her chest. Her mother had taught her well about which plants were edible and which were not. What most people saw as weeds, Trish saw as dinner. Putting her knowledge to work, she'd created a chickweed and dandelion green salad, along with sautéed purslane with strips of the leftover steak. Adding the freshly made biscuits resulted in a lunch fit for royalty.

"That's settled, then. I'm adding cooking to your responsibilities."

Bristling, Trish dumped her dishes in the sink. "Speaking of responsibilities, you hired me to help get this ranch back in working order, not clean your house or do your landscaping."

Dalton scooped up the last of the purslane and steak with a biscuit, then shoved it in his mouth and handed the dishes to Trish, who glared back at him. "For what I'm paying you, I don't think it's too much to ask."

"Oh really? And what's next? Taking care of your laundry? Washing your feet? Maybe you want me to be your own personal geisha?" Her anger at his remark was consuming her, and she knew she needed to stop herself, but his guarded expression sent her over the edge. She rolled her eyes. "A geisha is—"

"I know what a geisha is." The growl in his voice was unmistakable as he pushed away from the table and stood up. "So just what do you think your responsibilities should be?"

Trish moved to stand directly in front of Dalton, her hands on her hips as she looked up into his eyes. He'd given her the perfect opportunity to prove to him that she had the vision and passion to be his ranch manager, now and long into the future. "I want to make this the best damned horse ranch in the Midwest. I want our customers to be begging us for our horses and our competitors scrambling to keep up. I want the line of people trying to get in to see our horses to be so long that Bender has to build ten more hotels—and an airport! I want parents to bring their children here to learn to ride, and those children to grow up to be our hand-picked trainers. I want getting a place in that bunkhouse to be something people work their whole lives to achieve. When people think of this ranch, they are going to think of a family-friendly equestrian facility that offers the absolute best of the best. And my responsibility is to do anything and everything it takes us to get there."

Dalton grabbed her shoulders and pulled her up to him, kissing her hard on the lips before dropping her back down to the floor. "I knew you were the one." He squeezed her shoulders once again, his eyes sparkling with excitement. "So let's get to it."

He pushed past her and headed for the door. Trish was grateful that he hadn't noticed her clutching at the table for support. His kiss had been anything but sensual, but she had felt it down to her toes.

"Oh, but Trish?"

Turning, she saw him standing in the doorway. "Yes?" Her voice was barely a squeak.

"When I'm not here, you'll do what I tell you, even if it means cleaning my house or doing my laundry."

The door slammed behind him, and Trish was slammed back to reality, her anger flaring back to life.

They spent the rest of the afternoon working on the bunkhouse in silence. Trish painted while Dalton ripped out the old fixtures in the bathroom and replaced them with the new ones he had purchased in town. The sun had long set by the time they were done, and Trish was so exhausted she thought she would collapse where she stood, but she now had a functioning bathroom.

"I'll get out of your hair so you can get some rest."

"Hmm? Oh, yes." She stifled a yawn. "My bedroll awaits." She stretched her arms out, wincing at the pain in her back.

Dalton lowered his head and walked out of the bunkhouse.

Closing the door after him, Trish shook her head. "Well goodnight to you too. Honestly, I don't understand that man." She considered taking a hot shower before bed, but realized she was just too tired and settled on washing her face and brushing out her hair before changing into the tank top and shorts she used for pajamas. Within minutes, she was cuddled up in her bedroll, Traitor snoring at her feet.

The door flung open, startling Trish awake. When she sat up to see what had woken her, she saw Dalton standing in the doorway, carrying a mattress. He stared at her, the shock on his face suddenly turning into something else. *Desire?*

"Sorry, I didn't realize you'd already be sleeping." He nodded to the mattress. "Especially without this." He hefted the mattress into the frame, then helped Trish move the blankets to the bed.

"You make a girl positively swoon with delight, sir." She'd meant it to sound playful, but in her tired state her voice sounded sultry instead, and when Dalton turned in her direction, the look in his eyes knocked the breath from her.

He stepped closer to her. "Jesus, you're beautiful."

It was a whisper, a rush of air that set her blood on fire. Her mind was screaming at her to step back, put some distance between them, but her body was aching to put her arms around him and pull his body to hers. A vision of him stepping out of the creek, his naked body sleek and muscular, came to mind and she moaned, deep in the back of her throat.

He was kissing her before she could break the spell between them, but she knew she didn't want this spell to break. His kiss was driven, passionate, almost brutal, and she was afraid she would be carried away by his intensity. Actually, she hoped she would be carried away. She leaned into him, snaking her arms around his neck to pull him closer, until she felt the muscles of his chest pressed against her tightened nipples. He swept her up, never breaking contact, and placed her gently on the bed before joining her. She felt his hand lift her tank top and slide under, his palm burning a path to her breast. He kneaded it gently, then rubbed his thumb back and forth over her nipple until Trish moaned against him. He pulled away to lean down over her breast, kissing it through the fabric of her top. She pulled at the neckline, exposing her breast to his tongue and teeth, which continued their assault until Trish thought she would pass out from pleasure.

"Dalton, please!" The moan that escaped her lips sounded nothing like her voice. When Dalton lifted his head to look into her eyes, she knew she could not hide her desire. She didn't care. She wanted him, to feel him deep inside her. Tomorrow she'd be responsible. Tonight she'd let her body make all the decisions, and her body wanted him. All of him.

"Shit!"

The warmth left her as Dalton pulled away and stood up, stepping away from her bed and running his hands through his hair.

"I'm so sorry, Trish. That was way over the line. I—I...It won't happen again."

He walked out of the bunkhouse, slamming the door behind him just as Trish shrieked and threw her boot at the door. "Damn you, Dalton James!"

Chapter Ten

He heard her shriek and winced. Pausing on the porch, he contemplated going back inside to explain, to apologize for not being able to control himself, but there was the rub. If he saw her right now, in her thin tank top and tiny shorts that accentuated her long legs, he didn't think he could stop himself. And if she looked at him again with those heavy-lidded blue eyes, eyes that took on a much smokier color in the heat of passion, he knew he would do anything to have her. Knowing that she wanted him made it all the more painful to force his legs to move, carrying him as far from her as they could.

His father's laughter erupted in his ears once again. It was a sound that seemed to haunt his every waking moment and many of his sleeping ones. Randall James would have never let anyone distract him from his goals, especially a woman.

"Except my mother," Dalton growled as he entered the main house, "whom you sent away to avoid her distractions." That seemed to silence the mocking voice in his head. For now, at least.

Dalton swore to himself. He would never shun Trish just because he couldn't control himself. He would never be that weak.

He would just resign himself to a lot of cold showers.

For the next several weeks, Dalton pretended that nothing had happened between them. To Trish's credit, she did the same. They worked together but made little eye contact and spoke even less, which meant they made great strides in getting things done. The stable was cleaned out and repaired, sturdy fencing was installed over several acres to create various paddocks, and more of the weeds were cut back, although that task would be a never-ending chore. Dalton should have been thrilled by the progress, especially when they finished building a corral and replaced all the rotting posts in the training ring. Instead, his mood worsened with each passing day.

Each step toward getting the ranch up and running brought him one step closer to hiring a foreman to oversee the ranch's daily operations. Something told him that Trish would not appreciate not having the run of the place. He'd hire Trish for the job— certainly she was the most qualified—but Miranda had proved to him that the locals didn't like women in management. Besides, Trish was too friendly. The guys would eat her alive.

Deep down, he knew that she would leave rather than work for a foreman. That realization did not sit well with him.

He glanced over at her sitting on the fence while he worked Cyrus in the ring. She was already invested in the ranch, pointing out ways to incorporate trails crossing the entire property and improve the layout of the training rings. She took Traitor on hikes, returning with sketches of areas for trail development. He'd find her sketched ideas, with notes and arrows clarifying how they fit together, on the kitchen counter. Her ideas showed an understanding of horses and riding not evident among even the more experienced ranchers he had worked with. He appreciated her keen eye, but it irritated him that she could slip into the house without his knowledge. She no longer ate in the house, choosing instead to cook on the hotplate she'd picked up during one of her few trips into town. On Sundays she'd use the washing machine, but the notes were never left on Sundays, only during the week, which meant that at some point she slipped away from his watchful gaze.

Meaning there were at least a few times during the week when Bruce could get to her.

The afternoon sun was bearing down on him, making sweat run down his back. He removed his shirt and tossed it over the fence before he started lunging Cyrus. The horse was glistening as well, but he seemed to want to show off for his captive audience. Dalton couldn't argue with the animal. Trish was watching them with focused appreciation, and he reveled in the attention.

No, he didn't want her to leave, but according to Jake, it might be the only solution at this point. His friend left periodic messages about Bruce's behavior and his attempts to locate Trish. Jake was confident that he hadn't found her, but the man wasn't giving up. Dalton wondered if Bruce was just putting on a show. While repairing some fencing, he found several areas that were cut or ripped out entirely just days after being repaired. Could Bruce have found Trish but just be pretending that he hadn't? If Bruce was stupid enough to come onto his property, Dalton was going to give him exactly what he deserved.

He finished with the lunging, then walked Cyrus to the barn to let him cool down. Trish joined him to help brush the horse down.

"Your friend's not too happy." Dalton nodded at Traitor, who sat in the middle of the stable, far from the horse, which also meant he was far from Trish and Dalton. His whining was just loud enough to cause Cyrus to look at him and shake his head before stomping twice.

"Neither is yours."

They worked in silence for several minutes. Dalton frowned when she moved to the other side of the horse, going out of her way to avoid touching him while they brushed the animal. He gritted his teeth, realizing that what he was about to ask was not going to go over well.

He cleared his throat. "I need to make a run up to North Dakota."

She stopped brushing to look over Cyrus's back, and he saw the corner of her mouth curl in a subtle smile.

"And you're coming with."

The smile disappeared. She started brushing again. "No."

Now it was his turn to stop brushing. "Excuse me?"

"No." She didn't look up at him, even when he walked around Cyrus to glare down at her.

"Funny, I thought I was the boss here."

"Then maybe you should act like one."

He didn't know what that was supposed to mean and didn't really care, but the fact that she refused to look at him enraged him to the point that he no longer trusted himself around her.

"Enough," he hissed. "Just enough. Get away from him—and me." He snatched the brush from her and led Cyrus to the stable, telling himself to calm down as he walked away. His admonishments made him seethe. The woman was driving him mad. As he stabled Cyrus, he decided to give her a piece of his mind and tell her exactly how he felt.

But when he stormed back out of the stable, she was gone.

Chapter Eleven

When the bunkhouse door flew open, Trish looked up, startled. She was sitting at the small table Dalton had found for her, trying to make sense of his words. Now he stood in her doorway, his face twisted into an ugly scowl. Well, ugly for Dalton. He was still shirtless, the sweat from his workout with Cyrus accentuating the muscles straining across his chest.

If his stance weren't enough to warn her that he was angry, the fury in his eyes left no doubt.

He wouldn't harm her, even in his angriest state. Well, she didn't think he would. He was one of those people who just needed to get things off his chest, then the anger would pass.

She didn't bother to stand up. "Go ahead, do your worst."

It was the wrong thing to say, she realized, when a hurt look flickered across his face. His shoulders dropped, and he unclenched his fists.

"Don't ever do that—disappear like that."

She stared at him for a second. It registered in the back of her mind that he was struggling to keep his voice calm, but even that piece of information couldn't stop her from laughing so hard that she doubled over. She stood up, gasping for air, but when she looked back up at him, the laughter started again.

He stepped closer to her. "Dammit, I'm serious."

When she put her hand on his upper arm to reassure him, he flinched, but she didn't remove it. She was still chuckling when she replied. "Dalton, you have to make up your mind."

His brows furrowed in confusion, which made her laugh once again. He scowled, waiting for her to calm down.

Finally she was able to maintain a more or less serious tone. "You can't send me away then get angry that I left."

"I'll get as angry as I damn please when you just vanish like that!"

She bit the inside of her cheek to keep from laughing again.

He let out an exasperated sigh and ran his hand through his hair. "Look, I've been noticing some things."

"Things?" She crossed her arms, suddenly feeling defensive.

He shrugged, but wouldn't look her in the eye. "Cut fences. Missing tools."

She eyed him for a long moment. He was genuinely concerned, which caused Trish to frantically review everything she'd seen the last few weeks. Had something stood out? Been out of place? Been cause for alarm? While hiking the property, she always had a feeling of being watched. She assumed it was Dalton monitoring her while she explored. Although unnerving, she couldn't fault him for it. He was her employer, after all, and he was never overly obvious about it. But what if that feeling of being watched was something else? Or *someone* else.

"And you think—?"

Dalton nodded. "He's been telling people he's going to find you."

Now it was her turn to look confused. She shook her head. "That's not how Bruce operates. If he knew where I was, he'd make himself known."

"Not if he knows what's good for him."

His growled words sent an exhilarating tremor down her spine, and she warned herself to stay focused. But she couldn't stop her memory from flashing back to her powerful response to him just a few weeks ago. Since that night, she had analyzed the experience from seemingly endless perspectives, ultimately concluding that her response had simply been a reaction to everything that had brought her to the ranch. Dalton not only saved her from a distressing situation, but also offered her a chance at the life she'd always dreamed of as a ranch manager. Naturally there would be feelings of appreciation and excitement, and those had somehow translated into physical and emotional excitement. It didn't hurt that Dalton was a very handsome man, the kind of handsome that young girls drooled over and many women tended to avoid, knowing how much trouble it invited from other females trying to win over the affections of such a prized specimen.

"Look, we'll only be gone a couple of days."

His comment snapped her back to the present, but it did little to calm her.

"So you expect me to be glued to your side—what, for the rest of my life? Is that it?" She shook her head. "No, I won't let him run me off. I can take care of myself—and Bruce, if he's really that dumb."

Dalton opened his mouth to argue, but she held up a hand to cut him off.

"I'm not going to be controlled by anybody—not Bruce, not you, not anybody. Besides, you'll need someone to take care of Cyrus while you're gone?"

"I've already arranged for someone to check on him."

"Who?"

He shook off the question. "Look, you're coming with me, even if I have to tie you up and drag you into the truck."

"You will do no such thing, Mr. James." She knew using his surname would intentionally antagonize him. She hoped it would distract him, but it didn't work, and she found herself having to stand her ground, returning his icy stare. It was the wrong approach to take as her desire surged to life. She looked away before she did something stupid, like throwing herself at him and begging him to take her—and she wasn't thinking of North Dakota. She shrugged in what she hoped was a nonchalant manner. "Just postpone the trip."

He took a step closer to her, forcing her to look up at him. Trish held her breath, wondering if he would kiss her again and terrified that he wouldn't.

"This discussion's not over." He turned and stormed out, slamming the door behind him.

It turned out the discussion was over, as the next morning Dalton was gone by the time she got up. She headed for the main house, carrying an armful of clothes to be washed. Sitting in the kitchen, she was halfway through her first cup of coffee when she decided to explore the main house. Dalton had never offered her a tour, and she'd only been in the mudroom and kitchen area. She stepped through the swinging kitchen door out into a hallway that passed a richly carpeted staircase and ended at the front door. The large wooden door had an oval piece of etched glass in its center. To either side of the front door were large rooms. Both had beautifully stained floors and wood trim, but they were completely devoid of furniture.

"Guess he doesn't entertain much," she said to Traitor, who followed along at her heels. She headed upstairs, the puppy bounding ahead of her, where she found an L-shaped hallway and five doors. Three doors led to empty rooms with the same beautiful wood trim and floors as downstairs. Another door opened into a tastefully decorated bathroom.

Opening the fifth door, she gasped. The room was twice as big as the other bedrooms and was clearly the master bedroom. A large sleigh bed was positioned against one wall and on top of a plush Turkish carpet that covered almost the entire floor. Noticing two other doors in the room, she tiptoed across the rug and opened the first one, which revealed a master bath that would make royalty jealous. The room was tiled in soft whites and blues. A glass shower was on one side, and the biggest claw-foot bathtub she'd ever seen was on the other. It looked big enough to fit several people comfortably. She caught a hint of lilac soap and chuckled at the thought of Dalton, all serious and muscled, relaxing in a bubble bath. When she opened the second door, it felt like her stomach dropped to her knees. The walk-in closet was filled with dresses, shoes, and handbags that only a very rich woman would have.

Trish closed the door and turned back to the bedroom. Dalton had never mentioned a wife, but this room suggested he was married to a woman who apparently wasn't interested in living with him—or perhaps not until the ranch was up to snuff. The clothes, the furniture, even the rug screamed upper class. A woman like that wouldn't live on a ranch unless it was thriving, and she certainly wouldn't get her hands dirty building it up with her husband.

Trish tried to swallow past the lump in her throat as she walked back down the hallway. *Dammit!* She had no right to be upset about this. So he was married—good for him. And good for her, too. Now Trish could bury her attraction to him even deeper. He was married, which meant he was off limits. She could focus on her job and not let any of her childish daydreams get in the way.

But then why had he kissed her? He didn't strike her as the cheating kind. And he always took her at her word. For him it was clearly a matter of trust. If he said he would do something, he did it. He expected others to be the same. A man like that doesn't cheat on his wife...does he?

She was halfway down the stairs when the dog stopped near the bottom step, growling toward the front door. Trish stopped, then heard a car. Was Dalton back so soon? The dog wouldn't be growling at him, and the car wasn't stopping but driving by the ranch slowly. Too slowly. She moved to the front door, looking through the large oval window to see a car stopped at the end of the lane. She pressed her face to the glass, trying to get a better view, but the car sped off, kicking up gravel in its hasty retreat.

Odd. It was the first car she had seen on River Road since arriving several weeks ago. Dalton's warning came back to her, and she shivered.

"Oh, don't be such a ninny. So someone drove by? Big deal."

But she spent the rest of the day in the kitchen, cooking meals for the upcoming week and listening for the car to drive by again.

By dinner time she was getting cabin fever and chastising herself for letting a car spook her. The kitchen was broiling from her cooking marathon, and opening the windows hadn't helped cool the temperatures. If anything, the humidity outside turned the house into a sauna. Finally, she couldn't take it anymore. She left the puppy in the bunkhouse, despite his incessant howling, grabbed a change of clothes, saddled Cyrus, and headed out to the creek. A quick trip to cool down and she'd be back safe and sound in the bunkhouse without anyone knowing. Cyrus was all too happy to get out and stretch his legs a bit, and Trish gave him as much lead as he wanted. He was just as anxious as her to get to the creek.

The water was as cool and refreshing as she remembered, and she didn't want to leave. She decided to rinse out her hair as well, which cooled her down even more. But soon Cyrus was stomping his foot at her.

"Fine, fine, I'm coming." She stepped out of the water and gathered her things. "You're just as impatient as he is, you know that?"

When they came over the last hill, she could see the ranch buildings spread out before them in the distance. She also saw a truck sitting in the lane. Dalton's truck.

"No, no, no!" She gritted her teeth and steeled herself for his anger.

Cyrus felt her anxiety and picked up speed as they made their way along the path to the stable. The sun was dropping lower in the sky behind them, creating all sorts of stretched-out shadows along the path. Trish tried to rein Cyrus in, but he fought her. Dalton was at the end of the trail, and the horse could sense it. As they neared the stable, she saw Dalton saddling a regal Leopard Appaloosa. Is that why he went to North Dakota? The black and white horse whinnied, and Cyrus nickered in response. Dalton whipped around to glare at the incoming horse and rider.

"Damn it, Trish!" He grabbed Cyrus's lead and pulled Trish off the horse's back, holding on to her arm so tightly she thought he might break it. "You scared the hell out of me!"

"Dalton, you're hurting me." She tried to pull away, but he just held on tighter.

"Good, maybe it'll knock some sense into you!"

Trish's anger came screaming to the surface. "Oh, is that what you like to do? Hurt women?"

He shoved her away from him, scoffing in disgust. He led Cyrus to the stable, then returned for the Appaloosa. Trish stood watching, her arms crossed, barely holding in her temper. Finally, he locked up the stable and walked across the corral, his strides long, even, and angry.

"I don't get you sometimes." His voice was tight, like he was using every effort not to yell at her.

"Ha!" Trish threw her head back. "That's the pot calling the kettle black."

"This isn't funny, Trish." He moved a step closer until she had to look up to see his face. "I just drove nearly twelve hours round trip, not stopping for breaks and barely stopping for fuel, because I didn't want you to be alone here."

She felt the anger drain from her. He was genuinely concerned about her safety. Her shoulders slumped, and she took a step back, putting up her hands in surrender.

Dalton's anger was still brewing just under the surface, and her grabbed her by the upper arms and pulled her closer to him. "Your ex? He's been telling everyone in town that when he finds you, you're gonna pay for leaving him."

She tried to brush Dalton's hands away. "I told you, it's not him. Bruce is too lazy to hike through acres of land just to snip some wire. I'm not worried about him."

"Maybe you should be. When a man can't have what he truly wants, he'll do desperate things."

His voice was huskier now, still laced with anger, but she could hear his desire as well, the same desire she'd heard in his voice in the bunkhouse. A powerful urge to placate him welled up inside her.

"Okay, Dalton. I'm sorry." She pressed her hands against his chest, keeping her voice calm. "I promise, I will not do anything stupid."

"Good. Because you're not leaving this ranch—or my sight—until he calms down."

"What?!" The shriek in her voice startled the horses in their stables, and she heard them nickering repeatedly. "You do not own me, Mr. James." The ice in her tone could have frozen a lake in July. "And I'll be damned if I'm going to be your prisoner here."

"You're my employee living under my roof. I will not have your...your recklessness put my ranch in danger."

"You're just like Bruce," she hissed. "Worse!"

"Trish—"

She cut off his warning with a wave of her hand. "Send my wages for the week to the hotel. Good luck with your ranch, Mr. James." Her calm walk into the bunkhouse did not betray the seething anger she felt for this man, but her haphazard packing of her belongings did, especially once the tears started to fall. "Dammit! Pull it together, girlfriend." When she went back outside, Dalton was gone. Along with the keys to her truck.

Chapter Twelve

Dalton sped down the middle of the gravel road. The tires of his truck lost traction as he turned onto the crossroad. He held his breath when the tires skidded, waiting to see if they'd find their hold or he'd end up in the far ditch. It would be the perfect ending to his already miserable day.

But he had another plan in mind for ending this day.

As if approving his thoughts, the tires suddenly grabbed hold, and the truck lurched forward. He knew he was not thinking clearly. He'd gotten up at 4 a.m. to get on the road—not that he'd been sleeping before that.

Pulling onto the highway that led to town, he twisted his head first one way, then the other, trying to work out the stiffness in the back of his neck. Driving all day had been reckless, and the irony of his actions wasn't lost on him. He'd tried to postpone his trip, but the seller refused, and Dalton knew the horse was perfect for Trish. The fact that it had a lineage that made it worth three times the asking price only sweetened the deal. The seller owed his father for helping him with a cattle deal several years back, which was why he initially agreed to Dalton's low offer, but he had another buyer lined up and refused to pass up the opportunity if Dalton didn't show.

Making the drive alone turned out to be one of the smartest moves Dalton had made in a long while. It gave him time to think without being interrupted by thoughts of a certain blond. He'd come to realize he'd been wrong to demand that Trish come along with him. She was right. She could take care of Bruce. She had survived just fine before Dalton had come along and would undoubtedly continue to survive long after he was gone from her life.

He jerked the steering wheel, sending the truck careening into the bar parking lot. He parked in the first empty space he found and slid out of the truck, pocketing both his keys and Trish's.

The problem was, he didn't want her to leave. Not yet, anyway. In fact, he seriously hoped that the horse would be enough to convince her to stay on at the ranch, even after he hired a manager. She certainly knew horses. Even Cyrus liked her. Dalton had decided to put her in charge of the horses and hire a manager to oversee the other ranch hands. By the time he'd gotten back to Nebraska, he'd even managed to convince himself that she'd be thrilled with the offer.

When he returned to the ranch to find the dog locked up in the bunkhouse and Trish nowhere to be found, he'd almost called the sheriff in a state of panic. Then he noticed that Cyrus was gone, and he knew his horse would not go willingly if it sensed any kind of danger, even with Trish at the reins. His panic erupted into fury when he saw her ride over the hill, and it had taken every ounce of self-control not to ride out to meet her. He now knew that doing so would have been suicide, for it was not anger that fueled his fury, but fear.

He pulled open the bar door and stepped inside, waiting for his eyes to adjust. There was only one way to eradicate his fear when it came to Trish, and the answer was sitting on a barstool, three-quarters through his draft beer. Dalton sat next to him, ordered a shot of vodka with a beer chaser, then turned to face him.

"Hello, Bruce."

Chapter Thirteen

Trish sat on the bunkhouse porch in the dark, her shotgun across her lap. She only had one shell for the shotgun, the rest still packed in a box in the back of her truck. But the recipient of her ire didn't have to know that. One shot would be all she needed.

It had been hours since Dalton left her stranded, and during that time her anger had gone even deeper. It was now a quiet anger, the dangerous kind. She knew she wasn't thinking straight, but she didn't care.

About an hour after Dalton left and the sun had fully set, the strange car had driven by again. No lights were on in either the house or the bunkhouse, and the moon was just starting to rise over the horizon, so she didn't think they could see her sitting in the shadows. Trespassing was a serious offense in cattle country, even for a property with no cattle. She knew the law would be on her side if she had to fire at someone.

It was well after midnight when the car drove by a third time, but this time it pulled just into the lane and stopped, training its lights on the stable in the distance. Trish shifted deeper into the shadows as the car flashed its brights on and off. Inside the bunkhouse, she could hear Traitor doing his whine–growl combination. Luckily, no one in the car would hear it over the loud motor, which made Trish want to cover her ears.

The passenger door slowly opened, but no light came on inside the car. Whoever it was, they didn't want to be seen, and they had taken the appropriate precautions. Even the front license plate was obscured in the darkness, covered in mud or removed entirely. She couldn't tell. This did not bode well. Trish lifted her shotgun as someone stepped from the passenger side.

The individual never actually got out of the car. Trish saw the person turn back to the car, then raised voices. The person was suddenly back inside the car, the car door slammed shut, and the car reversing out of the lane at full speed. She lowered her gun slightly, still not convinced that they wouldn't try something else. As the car whipped out onto the road, she wondered what could have sent them scurrying. Had they seen her? The porch was in complete darkness.

She could barely see the bench sitting just opposite the bunkhouse door from where she sat.

A moment later, headlights flashed in the distance, and she realized that they had been scared off by another car coming down the road.

But the newcomer wasn't a car, it was a truck. Dalton's truck, in fact, and it was slowly weaving down the road. The truck careened from one ditch to another, and Trish realized something was wrong. At the lane, the truck turned, but not enough and Dalton drove into the ditch, then kept going several yards.

What the hell was he doing?

Several minutes passed. Nothing happened. What if he was hurt? What if the people in the car had somehow hurt him when they passed him? Her heart in her throat, Trish started to walk out to the truck when the driver-side door opened and Dalton fell out, yelling. No, not yelling. He was...singing?

Trying to stand up, he tripped over his own feet and fell into the grass, laughing.

"Well, Dalton James," she mumbled. "You drunken ass. Serves you right."

She turned and walked into the bunkhouse, determined to leave him passed out in the grass. After getting angry at her and stranding her here, he'd driven off in a fit...to get drunk. Trish leaned back against the door and chewed on her lip while she considered the latest turn of events. She went for a ride while he was gone, but he'd left her alone—supposedly the very thing he was afraid of. His anger stemmed from fear—it had to. Her luck wasn't great, but no one was so unlucky that they'd escape one controlling relationship only to fall into another right away. Not that she was in a relationship with Dalton, but hell, other than Cyrus and the pup, he was the only one she had talked to in weeks. That thought caused her to pause.

Had she really gone weeks without talking to anyone else?

Trish brushed the idea, and all implications, away and set the shotgun by the door so it'd be in easy reach, then changed into her sleeping clothes. She wouldn't leave tonight. No, she'd wait until tomorrow morning, when she could talk to him. The idea that he would go and get drunk when he was angry at her didn't sit well with her. Not at all. But one more night meant she could gloat while she sprayed ice cold water on him to wake him up. She almost laughed out loud at the thought, then stopped.

What if the car came by again? What would they do if they found Dalton passed out in the ditch?

Trish shook off the shudder she felt, slipped on her shoes, and went back outside. The truck door was still wide open, the headlights still on, and the motor still running, but Dalton was gone. She raced out to the truck, turning off the motor and closing it all up, then followed the path through the grass where he had stumbled—dragged himself?—toward the house until all traces of him vanished.

"You looking for me?"

She yelped in surprise at his words. Dalton was sitting on the porch, his back pressed up against the door and his legs jutting out in front of him.

"Can't open it." He giggled.

She shook her head and stomped up the steps. She leaned over to heft him up and nearly fell under his weight as he threw his arm around her shoulder.

"Good lord, did you drink the bar dry?"

"Yessiree we did!"

"So did you forget the back door opens right into your room—and without any steps?"

Dalton bellowed in laughter. "You're right. What a smart woman you are, Trish-a-licious."

She finally got the door open and helped him cross into the hallway, but Dalton lurched forward and swung around to look at her. "Now, hey there. Wait a just second. How do you know where's my room?" He tripped on his own foot and Trish put her arms out to hold him up again. "Have you been in my room?" His whisper nearly bowled her over with the smell of alcohol. "No, no." He pulled himself from her and spun around to walk down the hall. "I'd've remembered that, Trish-a-licious. Yes, indeedy." He turned into the kitchen.

Deciding he could survive the night fairly unharmed in his own house, although hoping he had a hangover to rival death warmed over, Trish was walking back through the front door when the sound of broken glass followed by a loud thud made her change her mind. Instead, she closed the front door and headed to the kitchen, where she found Dalton sprawled face down on the floor, broken glass spread out all around him.

She rolled him over, amazed to find no cuts. "What happened now?"

He giggled. "Swinging door hit me in the butt."

Trish hauled him to his feet again.

"I was gonna give it a piece of my mind, but the room got all spinny."

"Uh-huh. I bet it did."

They maneuvered around the glass shards and into his room. She turned on the light and led him to the bed.

"What did you do with your mattress, Dalton?"

"Gave it to my Trish-a-licious." He burped loudly and dropped to the box spring, which was the only thing left on the bed frame.

"Dalton James!" she screeched. "What the hell did you do tonight?" She knew she wasn't angry and him—

well, not this time. She was angry at herself for not realizing that he'd given her his mattress to sleep on.

"No. No, no, no." He leaned forward on the box spring, as if trying to get out of the bed, but he couldn't get the right leverage. Finally, he held his hand up, pointing at her. "Don't you call me that."

"Whatever." She reached over to turn off the light.

"No, wait!"

When Trish glanced back at Dalton, he was holding his legs straight out, pointing at his boots.

"You've got to be kidding."

"Can't reach 'em."

Trish rolled her eyes and straddled his leg to pull off the cowboy boot. "What is it with you and your last name, anyway? I've never met anyone who gets so angry at being called by their own name."

"Daddy issues."

Trish pulled the first boot off, then spun around to stare at him.

Dalton shook his head, then held his hand over his mouth, his eyes widening. The moment passed, and he nudged her with his other boot. Trish straddled his leg and started pulling.

"So what kind of daddy issues could you possibly have?"

"Mean. Mean son of a bitch." His voice a slurred growl, and when Trish got the second boot off and turned to look at him, his checks were flushed and his eyes narrowed.

She took an involuntary step back, then chastised herself. She knew he would never take his hatred and anger out on her. He was using those emotions to cover up the intense pain he felt—a pain she was all too familiar with. "You're nothing like that, Dalton," she whispered. She wanted to sit on the box spring with him, pull him into her arms, and hold him until he no longer felt the pangs of hurt, distrust, and guilt. "You'll never be him."

For a moment he stared at her, the anger washing away, taking his drunkenness with it. In that moment, Trish knew she was seeing the real Dalton, seeing his very core, a little boy trying to prove himself a grown man to a father who would never recognize him as such. Her heart shattered when she saw a child-like innocence reflected in his eyes.

But the moment passed when he burped a thank you to her, then somehow managed to scoot off the box spring and stand to shuffle to the door.

"Where do you think you're going?"

"Water. Thirsty." He pretended to cough, giving her a loopy smile.

"Sit. I will get you some water." Trish backed out of the room, giving him her best "don't mess with me" look. In the kitchen, she filled a plastic cup with water, then dumped half of it out. The last thing she needed was for him to spill water all over the place. Knowing her luck, he would spill it on himself and ask her to remove his clothes.

She needn't have bothered with the precaution. When she returned with the water, he was standing in the middle of the room, removing the very last stitch of his clothing by kicking his underwear off his wobbly, upraised foot and into a corner. He held up his arms in a show of victory.

Look away. It was the polite thing to do, the adult thing to do, but she was mesmerized by his muscles rippling from his chest down his abdomen and even lower. Suddenly, it didn't matter if he was her boss or not. Technically, he wasn't—her boss, that is. She'd quit. Although he was still married. Or was he? He wore no wedding band, he never spoke of a wife, and he had kissed her—on several occasions, no less! Such behavior didn't sound like that of a married man. He had put her in the bunkhouse, not the main house, but that would be natural for a working relationship, whether he was married or not.

He took a few steps toward her. Trish's heart pounded in her ears. Dare she take advantage of his inebriation to find out just how magnificent his body felt? Her body was reacting on its own, not caring about the debate in her head. It cast its vote and was ready for a night of wild abandon with Dalton James. He moved closer and Trish's mind was screaming at her, until Dalton reached out to take the water from her.

He gulped it down and handed the cup back to her. Trish let out the breath she'd been holding. She would put him to bed and walk away. She had to.

Before she could stop him, he reached his arms around her and pulled her into a tight embrace. She could feel every bit of him pressed against her body, her thin tank top and shorts offering no protection against his manliness. Her body renewed its efforts to take advantage of the situation. Dalton sighed, his warm breath tickling her neck. "I love you, Trish."

Trish desperately tried to keep her mind from reeling, telling herself it was just the alcohol speaking, that he wasn't in control of his faculties. But her brain was arguing that the alcohol meant that he had lost all inhibition and was saying what he truly felt, whether he would admit to it or not when he was sober. Her body decided to take action, and her hands slid up Dalton's back, discovering every swell and bulge of his muscles. Trish could still hear the voice in the back of her mind screaming at her, but she couldn't make out what it was saying as she inhaled Dalton's musky smell. She let her hands slide back down, going even lower to grasp his firm buttocks. She didn't care what was right or wrong anymore. She wanted this man. She *needed* him.

Dalton turned his face into her neck and made a muffled noise. He pulled back, giggling like a schoolboy. "That tickles." He turned away from her and crawled into bed, pulling a thin sheet up to his chin.

Trish's face burned with embarrassment. She stormed through the mudroom, slamming the door behind her, thankful that he was too drunk to realize what just happened. Well, almost happened.

After a night of tossing and turning in the bunkhouse, Trish finally gave up and decided to get up for the day. The sun hadn't lifted above the horizon yet when she left Traitor snoring in her bed and headed to the main house to make coffee and cause a little mischief of her own. Determined not to let his treatment of her just a few hours earlier go without retaliation, and ignoring the little voice that reminded her that he was not in control last night and had no idea how he'd embarrassed her, Trish was ready to pull out all the stops. If she was going to have to suffer through her attraction to him, then he could suffer a bit as well. She figured some ice water dumped on his head would be a nice way to start his Monday.

Dalton was already sitting on a stool at the counter, dressed only in a pair of faded jeans, his bare feet propped up on the stool's rungs and his face buried in his hands.

Frustrated that he'd thwarted her plan already, she sang out a "good morning" as loudly as she could. Dalton groaned. Trish smiled. "My, my, you're up awfully early, especially after such a work out last night."

Dalton shifted his head so he could look up at her with one eye that squinted against the light. "Huh?"

She was about to explain how he'd parked the truck and had to drag himself through the grass, but another idea quickly formed in her mind. She winked at him as she ran a hand over his shoulder and down his arm, giving his bicep a little squeeze. "Don't you remember, sweetheart?" She shifted to stand behind him and pressed her body against his back. "It was earth-shattering," she whispered. "Your word, by the way."

Dalton dropped his arms to the counter, pressing his forehead into them. Trish bit her lip to keep from laughing. This was going to be just too much fun.

She flipped on the coffee maker, scrambled several eggs, and toasted thick slices of bread, which she put on a plate and slid across the counter to Dalton. He was watching her now, several emotions struggling on his face: disbelief, fear, and something that made his eyes light up—*delight?* But just as quickly as that last emotion arrived, he tamped it back down with a look of frustration.

Trish placed a cup of coffee on the counter next to his plate, then leaned over the counter, propping her chin in her elbows. "Don't tell me you don't remember anything?" She frowned and blinked several times, giving him a petulant pout that she'd seen other women use on their men when they wanted something. "I must not have been good enough, then." Shuffling around the counter and past him, she hung her head low as if devastated by this news. It took every ounce of control not to burst out laughing.

She was just about to yell "gotcha" when he grabbed her elbow and spun her around to face him.

"I'll damn sure remember this time."

His lips were on hers before she could push him away—tell him it was all a joke and laugh about it. The kiss deepened, intensified, and instead of trying to resist, her hands slid up his chest and around his neck. He wanted her, and there was no way she could stop him. Luckily, she didn't want to.

Her desire burst from the walls she'd built to keep it in check, and she moaned as every cell of her being seemed to become aware of Dalton, his tight muscles, his earthy smell, his manly taste. She pulled back just enough to pull open her button-up shirt, desperate to press her own flesh against him. Dalton realized what she was doing and pulled at the edges of her shirt so hard that the buttons fell to the floor. In that same instant, he grabbed her waist and lifted her onto the counter, giving him easier access to her throat and breasts while she wrapped her legs tightly around him.

His hands slid down her neck, followed by his hot kisses, his tongue creating a burning trail to one of her nipples. Trish groaned as he pulled her bra down to give his tongue full access to the hardened nub. She arched her back into his kisses, which moved lower to her abdomen. She fell back on the cool counter of the kitchen island, her fingers tangled in Dalton's hair, pulling him closer to her. He moved back to her other nipple, and Trish opened her mouth to beg him to take her now, but instead she let out a loud gasp as his fingers moved between her legs. She hadn't felt him unzip her shorts or slide his hand into her panties, but she wouldn't have stopped him if she had, especially not now, knowing how he was driving her body crazy with desire. She had never wanted anything so badly in her life. She wanted to have him inside her. Now.

"Well, now, Dalton," a female voice said behind him, bringing his assault on Trish's body to a sudden halt. He glanced up to lock eyes with Trish as the female voice said, "Is this how we're paying the hired help these days?"

Chapter Fourteen

"That is such a delightful way to reduce costs, isn't it?"

Dalton held Trish in place, her shirt spread open, his hand still in her shorts. He didn't turn around to look at the intruder, instead keeping his stare firmly on Trish, who struggled to pull her clothes back on. But the more she struggled, the harder he pressed his hips into hers, pinning her into place. He knew he was hurting her, could tell by the pinched look in her face, and he wished he could explain why, but right now he focused only on keeping her still and protecting her from the other woman.

"What do you want, Miranda?"

Waiting for her reply, he clenched his teeth so tightly he felt stars at the corner of his vision. He needed to stay calm. When Miranda smelled fear, she went for blood. He stared at Trish, trying to remain focused. If anyone could handle Miranda, it would be Trish, but he wasn't ready to witness that cat fight.

"Dalton, sweetie, is that the way it's going to be?"

He felt the black rage descend over him, but was powerless to stop it. *Sweetie?* She was really laying it on thick today.

Trish pushed against Dalton. "Let go," she hissed. He held her more firmly.

"Hmm, seems like this little trifle isn't as willing as your past conquests."

Trish's neck and cheeks burned red hot, and her fingernails dug into Dalton's arms, causing him to flinch. It was just distracting enough that Trish could push him back and slide off the counter, pulling her blouse around her to face the woman who dared called her a *trifle*.

Dalton moved between the two women. Trish's disheveled appearance was no comparison for the tall, platinum blond woman dressed in a sleek black power suit that accentuated her feminine curves perfectly. He knew Miranda's large ruby pendant, designer bag, and the power heels were all carefully orchestrated to make those around her feel inferior. She took no prisoners. Ever.

"Well, my, my, you are quite the beauty, aren't you? And able to outmaneuver Dalton? A rare find indeed." Her voice was like honey: sweet and gooey. Dalton wasn't fooled for a second. She stuck her hand out in greeting, flashing a giant diamond ring on her left hand. "Mrs. Miranda James."

Trish spun around to fix Dalton with an icy stare. "Married? Really?" She scoffed at him in disgust. "You're worse than Bruce."

Trish's pushed past him. He wanted to reach out and stop her, to pull her to him and whisper the truth in her ear, but her last comment felt like a cold knife plunged deep into his gut, paralyzing him. He stood rooted to the spot while he listened to her storm down the hallway, slamming the front door behind her.

Miranda's quiet chuckling snapped him back to life. He glared at her, which made her laugh out loud.

"Just what do you find so damn funny?" He ground the question out.

"You, silly." Miranda threw an arm around his shoulder. "I've never seen you like this."

He shrugged her arm off and stepped away from her, trying to put distance between them. "Like what?"

"In love." She held up her hand to stop him from protesting. "Don't insult me with your excuses."

Dalton placed both hands on the counter, as if holding himself up. In reality, he didn't want Miranda to see his face. He'd never been able to hide anything from her, and she'd been merciless in her torment of him. Still was, in fact. And now she knew about Trish. He swore under his breath. He should have come clean with Trish, told her everything about his family. Now it was too late—all because of Miranda.

He stood and turned toward her, his face a mask of hardened determination, but Miranda was gone. He stepped into the hallway and saw her standing on the porch, the front door wide open behind her.

"Miranda—"

"You better hurry." She didn't even turn to face him.

"I don't know what game you're playing—"

She looked at him now, rolling her eyes in the process. "Look, we both suck at relationships, so any advice I give you is like the blind leading the blind."

"But?"

Miranda arched a thin eyebrow at him. "A beautiful woman who's not afraid to stand up to you?" She sighed. "And by the looks of this place, she's not afraid of hard work, either."

Dalton crossed his arms and frowned. He wouldn't give Miranda any more ammunition. Instead, he stared out across the ranch, realizing with a start that it actually was a ranch and no longer a ranch-in-the-making. In a matter of weeks he and Trish had brought the abandoned property back to a place where it could be a functioning ranch. All it needed now were horses. And Trish.

"You know, Dalton, I've only seen that expression on your face one other time."

He looked at her from the corner of his eye. "Oh yeah?" He prepared himself for one of her barbs.

She nodded, then turned to look him in the eye. "Whenever you talk about your mother."

"So what are you saying?" He tried to sound gruff, but his voice was about as menacing as a kitten.

She shrugged, but she couldn't hide the knowing look on her face.

A few seconds later, Dalton was storming down the front steps and heading toward the bunkhouse.

"She's not there."

When he spun around to face Miranda again, she was pointing down the road.

"She left. Driving your truck, no less." This time Miranda didn't keep her laughter to herself.

Chapter Fifteen

Trish sped down the highway toward Bender, letting her anger seethe. The fact that Dalton still had her keys, forcing her to take his truck, made her grip the steering wheel so tightly her fingers hurt. She knew it wasn't healthy, but the anger kept the tears at bay, and she'd be damned if she was going to cry over Dalton James. Not when he had a wife. Was that why he'd been so adamant that she stay at the ranch when he was gone? So she wouldn't run into his wife in town? But clearly she lived at the ranch as well—or at least her belongings did—so that didn't make sense. And why hadn't he mentioned her? Not once. But Miranda said he'd had past conquests, so he was used to having his flings. He was probably so used to hiding his married life from all his "trifles" that it was second nature to him.

Trish frowned. Something didn't feel right. He knew she was attracted to him. He knew he could have had her that night in the bunkhouse, but he had stopped. Trish wasn't naive either. Stopping had not been what he wanted to do that night. Yet he'd done it, pulled away, even though he wanted her as much as she wanted him, as this morning's scene proved. Her lips were tender from the power of his kiss, and she could still feel his hands and tongue exploring her body, which was demanding satisfaction now that it had been aroused to such a state. So if he was supposedly having a fling, where was the fling?

Nearing town, she decided to head for the hotel in hopes of finding Jake. Jake had vouched for Dalton. The two were clearly friends, and Trish knew that Jake didn't vouch for anyone unless they were on the up and up. Jake was good people. No way would he have sent her from one viper's pit to another. Something just didn't add up, but for the life of her, she couldn't figure out what.

She parked the truck in the employee area. For a moment she rested her head on the steering wheel, desperately trying to sort through what was happening in her life. Finding a new place to live was supposed to have solved her problems, at least temporarily, giving her the freedom to move on and build the life she wanted. But moving out to the ranch had created even more problems—problems that were confusing her and churning up emotions that she fought to hide—and she felt even more trapped now than she did a month ago. She could leave Bruce. She could even leave Dalton. How was she supposed to leave her own broken heart?

She wiped at her eyes, making sure no tears had escaped, then climbed out of the truck. She locked the doors and threw the keys into the nearby ditch. She'd at least get even with Dalton for leaving her stranded yesterday.

"Trish?"

A shiver ran up her spine. She was only a few steps from the hotel's back entrance. Should she make a run for it? Would it make a difference? He'd just follow her.

"Hey, Bruce," she said, turning to face him as he walked up behind her.

"Dang, girl, I been looking all over for you. Where you been?"

He smiled as if they were long lost friends, but the smile didn't reach his eyes and Trish knew he was angry. Furious, even. She was in a dangerous predicament, made more so because, as she glanced around, she realized that no one could see them unless they actually pulled around to the back of the hotel.

"Oh, you know, working." Her calm voice surprised even her.

"Huh, I ain't seen you here for weeks."

He stood in front of her, close enough that if he decided to get violent with her, he could. He never had before, not with her, always taking his fury out on his friends or some poor guy caught at the wrong time in the wrong bar, but Trish knew—had always known, though she ignored it—that his violent nature would someday be focused on her. She'd always told herself that she'd leave him before it got that far, but now here they stood. She'd left him, but not yet escaped him. He'd been lying in wait while she walked right into his trap.

Glancing around one last time, hoping for something to help her avoid what was about to happen, she noted the security cameras pointed at the parking area. At least there would be proof she could use to press charges. If she survived.

Bruce stepped closer, lifting his hand to brush her hair back from her cheek. "Don't worry, they're not recording." He leaned in close to whisper in her ear. "I cut the wires."

Her skin turned cold despite the warmth of the morning sun. Bile rose in her throat, but she pushed it back down. She was alone with him, and no one was going to intervene to save her. Bruce's expression left no doubts in her mind. He meant to hurt her.

She'd just have to hurt him first.

Trish reached up to Bruce's upper arms, grabbing him to pull him closer. She raised her knee and connected as hard as she could to his genitals, then brought her foot back down, connecting her heel to his toes, mashing them into the cement parking lot. Bruce moaned in pain, grabbing her wrist in a vice-like grip as she tried to push him away.

When she heard him laughing, she froze.

"You missed, you stupid whore," he hissed. His grip moved to her throat, tightening as she thrashed at him with her still-free arm.

Bruce's eyes widened as he was lifted several inches off the ground, his face contorting in pain. He let go of Trish as he went sprawling backward onto the cement.

Dalton stood over him. "Recognize me, Bruce? My good old drinking buddy?" Dalton's arm pumped up and down as he punched Bruce repeatedly. "Last night I decided you were too pathetic to kill. Won't make that mistake again."

"Stop it!"

Dalton whirled on her, still holding Bruce to the ground. "Get in the truck!"

"Let him go!"

The black rage was etched into his face, his scowl, even his eyebrows, but it was the fury in his eyes that shocked her most. His normally caramel eyes were so dark they were almost black. He looked at her, and for a split second she wondered if he would take out his anger on her. The thought made her stomach churn in disgust. Dalton might have caused her emotional pain, but he would never hurt her physically.

"Don't do this, Dalton." She tried to keep the shriek from her voice.

"Get in the damned truck!"

She felt the sharp enunciation of each word as if it were a slap in the face. She stepped closer to him, putting her hand on his raised arm, feeling his anger rippling through his muscles. He sneered at her, an animal-like snarl that caught her breath.

"Dalton, please." Her voice was quiet, calm, soothing. She needed to break through his fury and reach the rational man inside. "You have to let him go. You have to let me deal with him."

"I'll never let him near you!"

"I know, I know." She placed her other hand on his fist, never breaking eye contact with him. "But if you care about me, if you have any feelings for me at all, you must let me deal with it."

She watched the beast struggle with the man, his face showing his internal strife. Finally, he made a disgusted sound and stood up, kicking Bruce as he did. Trish let out a ragged breath, moving to stand between Dalton and Bruce—or what was left of Bruce. His face was covered in blood and was already swelling into painful disfigurement.

"Bruce, can you hear me?"

His tried to speak through his puffy lips, then finally nodded his head, moaning at the effort.

"I do not belong to you. We are not together, and we never will be. You will stop trying to find me. No more waiting for me to show up at work or driving by my house, understand? We are done."

He nodded and moaned once more.

Trish thought for a moment, then added, "And if I ever even think you are following me, I am going to let Dalton loose on you—and I won't be there to stop him next time. Understand? Good, now get in your car and get out the hell out of here."

They watched Bruce pull himself up and half walk, half crawl to his car. Dalton had parked Trish's truck behind him, blocking him in, so Bruce drove up onto the sidewalk and across the small grassy area, taking out several planters and ambient lights in the process. Once he was finally out on the road and driving away, Trish turned to Dalton.

His eyes were still burning with emotion. She steeled herself for what she had to say.

"The same goes for you, Dalton. Leave me alone. I can't do this anymore. I can't work with you, can't be around you." Her voice caught in her throat, and she knew the emotions of the morning were catching up with her. She continued in a rush, afraid that if she didn't speak now, she wouldn't be able to speak at all. "I can't see you day in and day out, knowing that I can't have you. I don't trust myself around you, Dalton. I don't trust my feelings for you, and I am not going to be your trifle or your next conquest." The tears were streaming down her face now. She couldn't stop them.

Dalton stepped closer, until he was just inches from her. "Get in the truck, Trish." His words were barely a whisper.

She shook her head, saying "I can't!"

Dalton swept her up in his arms and placed her in the driver's side of her own truck, the motor still running. He slid in beside her, pushing her gently into the passenger seat, then backed out of the parking area.

"Dalton, why won't you listen to me?"

He looked at her, and Trish was shocked into silence at the concern she saw in his face. Concern, but something else, something so powerful that she felt her body instantly responding to him.

"I heard every word you said."

Chapter Sixteen

Dalton drove north of town, then headed west on the highway, passing the turn to the ranch.

"Where are we going?"

He ignored her question. "Why didn't you tell me he was driving by the house?" He kept his eyes on the road, both hands on the steering wheel, afraid to look at her.

Trish looked out her window and sighed.

He frowned. He could play the ignoring game too.

They drove several miles in silence. Dalton muttered under his breath, angry at himself for not being able to withstand a little silence. Finally, he whipped the truck off the road and turned to look at her, waiting. She avoided looking at him. He, on the other hand, could not look anywhere but at her.

"Fine." She glanced over at him. "I wasn't sure it was him, so I didn't want to say anything. And the more I think about it, the more I am sure it wasn't him. The only time I saw the car was when you weren't there, and he would have seen my truck and come looking for trouble."

"But someone was driving by."

She turned away from him once again. "Yes."

"And you didn't tell me."

"Nope."

Dalton gritted his teeth. "Why not?"

She looked at him, pursing her lips. "Because the first time I could have said anything, you were too busy yelling at me for not following your orders while you were out of town. And the second time, you were so drunk you fell out of your truck."

He winced at the comment, knowing he had so much to explain to her, but now was not the time. He leaned his head back against the headrest and closed his eyes. She was right. He'd been so concerned with keeping her at the ranch that he'd stopped talking to her. She wasn't keeping things from him out of fear. Rather, he'd made it impossible for her to share anything with him. That would have to change.

He rolled his head to the side to smile at her. "You could've told me today."

His words had the opposite reaction than he expected. She clenched her fists, then crossed her arms, as if to prevent her hands from throttling him. "I suppose I could have, between you kissing me, your wife interrupting us, and you beating my ex so badly he couldn't talk, but I just couldn't find the right moment."

He sat up so quickly, he wrenched his neck. He grimaced and grabbed his neck, trying to ease the pain.

"Ha, serves you right."

Her words held no venom. In fact, he thought he saw concern in her face before she turned to look out the window again. He massaged his neck with his fingers, trying to make sense of what she just said, then groaned inwardly when he realized what she thought of the situation. He started the truck once again, glanced at her, then pulled out onto the highway, trying to decide how to explain everything without her feeling like she'd been duped.

Chapter Seventeen

The fact that he didn't deny Miranda was his wife stung Trish, and she pouted in silence for several miles. She didn't want to think about it anymore, didn't want to be near this man and be constantly reminded of what a fool she'd been.

"Well?" she asked.

"Well what?"

"I answered your question, now you answer mine."

His thick eyebrows furrowed together as he tried to remember.

Trish rolled her eyes. "Where are we going?"

"Here." He nodded at a sign along the side of the road that said "Welcome to Harrington."

Trish shrugged, knowing she'd get no more from him. At least they were in a populated area. With nearly fifteen thousand residents, Harrington was the county seat and the largest town for almost an hour in any direction. It would be as good a place as any to end her association with Dalton once and for all.

When he parked the truck at the courthouse, she held her hand out. "Keys, if you don't mind."

He stepped out of the truck, dropped the keys in his pocket, then reached back in to grab her hand and pull her out. "I do mind. Very much." He pulled her close and held her, looking into her eyes in such a way that Trish's breath caught in her throat. He turned to walk into the courthouse, never letting go of her hand.

Once inside, Miranda James detached herself from a trio of elderly women whom Trish recognized as the Carter sisters. Trish nodded a greeting to them, and they waved back.

Meanwhile, Miranda nearly bowled Dalton over. "Well it is about time. I've had about as much as I can stand of 'Octogenarians Are Us.'" She glanced at the sisters, then back to Dalton and Trish. "What took so long?"

"Had to take care of some business."

Miranda noted Trish's scowl, then raised her eyebrow at Dalton.

"Tell her," he said.

"Tell her what, sweetie?"

"She won't listen to me." He pulled Trish forward, closer to Miranda. "Tell her who you are."

Miranda's smile spread across your face. "Now, Dalton, are you telling me you can't sweep her off her feet with those sweet-as-molasses eyes and your rural charm? I never thought I'd see the day."

"Just shut up and tell her."

Emotionally and physically exhausted from a night of no sleep and a morning full of drama, Trish couldn't handle any more games. "Dalton, don't do this. Just don't. I don't know what your game is here, but I want no part of it. Gimme my keys and you and the wife can be on your merry little way."

Miranda's laugh was cut short by Dalton's angry outburst. "Tell her!"

Trish jerked her hand from his. "Enough! If you have something to say, say it and be done, but don't put me in the middle of whatever sick games you two have cooked up."

"She's my sister."

Now it was Trish's turn to laugh. "You really think I'm that gullible? You don't know me at all, Mr. James."

He scowled at her, but she didn't back down. "How many times do I have to tell you? Don't call me that!"

"I'll call you any damn thing I please, *Mr. James.* You don't own me!"

"Excuse me," a man's voice said, interrupting them.

Trish and Dalton both turned to the voice, yelling "What?"

Sheriff Tate Trudell eyed them, giving them each a look that clearly said calm down, while Miranda giggled behind them. He paused to look pointedly at her, then at the Carter sisters, who had moved closer to watch the drama unfold. Finally, he returned to Trish and Dalton. "Do we have a problem here?"

"No, sir, we don't."

Trish crossed her arms and glared at Dalton. "Don't you dare answer for me!" She waited until he bowed his head almost imperceptibly in apology. "No, sheriff, no problems here."

The sheriff studied them once more, then placed a hand on Dalton's shoulder. "Dalton James?" When Dalton nodded, he continued. "Just got a call about you. Seems you roughed up a local in Bender?"

"I did, sheriff." He stared at Trish as he answered, but Trish refused to look at him, her arms still crossed tightly against her chest.

"Huh, well he's pressing charges, so I guess that admission will make it easy."

Dalton's stare never left Trish's face, while Trish continued to look at the sheriff. The idea of seeing Dalton hauled away in handcuffs made her almost giddy. She even tried to smile at him, although she was pretty sure it came off like a leering loon. Yet he still stared at her, and Trish was becoming increasingly uncomfortable.

"Okay, fine!" She rolled her eyes and let out a deep sigh. "Mr. James," she said, savoring how Dalton gritted his teeth at the use of the name, "actually stepped in to save me from Bruce Garrison, who at the time was attempting to strangle me."

"I always said that Mr. Garrison was a bad seed," Lily Carter said. Her sisters nodded in agreement.

Sheriff Trudell leaned in slightly to examine her neck, and Trish could still feel where Bruce's fingers had pressed into her skin. "I was hoping that night in jail had calmed him down a bit."

As the sheriff asked Trish a few more questions, verifying the details, she saw Miranda elbow Dalton. "Clearly the one. Does she know that?"

Dalton's eyes never left Trish. "We're about to find out."

The comment made Trish's knees feel like jelly, but she didn't know why.

"We'll need you to come down to my office to provide a statement," the sheriff said. "And I'll need to take some photos of your bruising." He glanced toward Dalton, resting his hand on the butt of the gun at his hip, then spoke to Trish in a quieter voice. "Everything okay here, Miss Cassidy?"

"Actually, there is something you can do for me." She said it loud enough for everyone to hear. She kept her eyes locked on Dalton. For a brief moment she considered telling the sheriff that she'd been kidnapped and taken against her will, but only for a very brief moment. Dalton's tight jaw and dark eyes told her she was already testing his limits. Another step could break him entirely. "Could you help me verify who this woman is? There seems to have been some confusion."

"Oh, you are a spitfire," Miranda said, approval evident in her voice.

Rose Carter clasped her hands to her chest and giggled. "My heavens, isn't she, though?"

"I told you. She's my sister." Dalton could barely speak, he was gritting his teeth so tightly.

When Trish stuck her tongue out at him, Dalton burst into laughter, startling both the sheriff and Miranda. Trish just rolled her eyes. "Like I would believe you."

The pained expression that flickered across Dalton's face cut through Trish's heart. It was just as quickly replaced with a guarded look.

Daisy Carter stepped forward. "Sweetie, he's telling the truth. Mrs. James here is truly his sister."

"But she's married."

Miranda laughed. "Surely you of all people understand the benefits of letting the cattlemen believe you're married? A single woman trying to do business with them? Please! If you're lucky they just dismiss you with a condescending pat on the head. More often than not, they try and marry you off to some third cousin. But a married woman, now that's a different story."

It took Trish just one look at Miranda for the truth to come crashing down, along with the realization that she'd just made an epic fool of herself. Stunned, Trish took a step back, nearly tripping on her own feet, but Dalton was there, catching her and steadying her against him. Dalton, who now was facing assault charges because she'd run off from his ranch in a snit, jealous of his sister—*his sister!* "I think I'm gonna be sick."

Dalton wrapped his arms around her and slowly rubbed one hand up and down her back. The rhythmic motion was calming, and she felt her frayed nerves returning to some semblance of normalcy.

A clerk stepped into the hallway. "Dalton James?"

He shifted, turning her toward the clerk and the open doorway while still letting her lean all her weight into him.

"Sheriff, can we finish up with you in just a bit? We've got some business here to take care of, but then we'll come right to your office."

A smile tugged at the sheriff's lips as he glanced at the pair before him. "Oh, I think I'll stay for this. It ought to be entertaining."

"Don't forget us." Lily pulled on Daisy's arm. "I wouldn't miss this for anything."

Dalton nodded. "Actually, I could use the witnesses."

Trish pushed away from Dalton and stumbled several feet into the courtroom before coming to a complete stop, blocking the others from moving forward. A judge stood in front of his bench, a book in his hand. He motioned them forward.

"What's going on?" she mumbled. She tried to turn around, leave the way she came, but Dalton was there, standing at her side.

"Marry me." The whisper in her ear sent shivers down her spine. Surely she had misheard him. She looked up at him, waiting for him to speak again, but he just watched her, his face still expressionless, his eyes still guarded. Was he serious? Where was this coming from?

Trish's insides melted as comprehension sunk in. "Dalton, this morning—us sleeping together, it was all a joke. I was joking. Nothing happened last night. You don't have to do this."

The bashful smile matched a light blushing in his cheeks. "I know." He bent down so only she could hear him. "I wasn't that drunk."

She stepped back to look at him, her anger flaring, but just as quickly she dismissed it. He played a joke on her, she played one on him. Only now they were in the courthouse getting married.

"Then why are we here?"

"You have feelings for me."

"So?"

"I have feelings for you too."

"That doesn't mean we should get married. I mean, we barely know each other. You don't marry someone you've only known a few weeks!"

Miranda called out, "She's got a point there."

Dalton scowled at her. "Butt out, sis."

"Listen to her," Trish said. "This is crazy. So we've got feelings for each other. Attraction doesn't equal marriage."

"Trish—"

"I mean, I don't know your religious views or your political views—and what if you snore? What if I snore?"

"Trish! Can I say something here?"

She blinked at him. After several seconds of silence, she opened her mouth to say something, but he put his hand up to stop her.

"I cannot envision life on the ranch—our ranch—without you. I want you by my side. I want to share my triumphs with you and my failures. I want you to help me grow this ranch into the success we both know it can be." He stepped closer, pulling her into his arms. "I want us to run it, together. I want to wake up with you in my arms and go to sleep with you snuggled up next to me. I want to drink your nasty coffee every day and swim naked in the creek with you, take horseback rides with you, and count the stars with you every night. I don't ever want to have to control myself when I am around you. I want to stop not getting sleep at night because all I can think about is you. I want to make love with you until we're both so exhausted we can't move...and then I want to do it again. I want to have babies with you: boys who have your strength and determination and girls who have your fearlessness and intelligence and wit. I want to build a life with you because I fell in love with you on a bench outside a hotel in a little town. Marry me. I know you think it is a risk, that it's not something you planned, but I promise I will spend the rest of my life proving to you that it was worth the risk."

The emotions swirling inside her made Trish light-headed, and she took a calming breath before looking back up into Dalton's eyes. "You don't like my coffee?"

It was Dalton's turn to roll his eyes before dropping his head so their foreheads touched. "Trish, please."

"Yes, I will marry you." She pulled him closer to her as she purred, "Mr. James."

Chapter Eighteen

Trish sat on the porch, drinking iced tea with the Carter sisters while Traitor slept at her feet. She suppressed a giggle, wondering how on earth the dog could sleep through the chattering. The trio of elderly ladies had followed Trish home from her impromptu wedding.

"I just can't believe that new sheriff," Rose said. "Arresting a man on his wedding day!"

"Without even giving you young people a chance to consummate the wedding." Daisy frowned, shaking her head.

"Ha!" Lily nearly spit out the tea she'd just sipped. "These young kids have probably consummated it ten times already."

Rose pursed her lips at her sister. "Lily, don't be so crude."

"Crude, schmude. I'm just stating the obvious." She set her glass of iced tea down on the table. "You think any man could withstand a beauty like Miss Cassidy here?"

"I believe her name is Mrs. James, now." Rose looked down her nose at Lily, who harrumphed loudly.

"Oh, but Mr. Dalton James is a mighty fine specimen." Daisy leaned forward slightly, as if sharing a secret. "Oh, please tell me he's as good between the sheets as I imagine."

Trish stared at the three women, unsure what to say. Jake Monroe's aunts were regulars at the hotel's Sunday brunch, and she was used to their outspoken nature, but usually she was laughing along with them, not being the focus on their microscopic inspection. "Well, what can I say?" Trish cleared her throat. "Except that a lady doesn't kiss and tell."

Daisy clapped her hands. "Oh, that means he is." She sat back in her chair, sighing loudly.

Trish pretended to fan herself from the heat, hoping the elderly women didn't notice the blush rising to her cheeks.

Rose laughed. "Now you've done it. She'll keep herself entertained all week with thoughts of Mr. James."

"I don't believe it!"

They all turned to look at Lily, whose face was scrunched into a ball of wrinkles as she stared at Trish.

"Nope, don't believe it all. Sisters, look at her." Lily turned to her sisters as she waved a hand toward Trish. "She's been about as intimate with Mr. James as Daisy here."

This time, Trish couldn't hide the embarrassment burning her face.

Daisy let loose a disheartened sigh while Rose clucked her tongue in disapproval. Lily continued to frown.

"Oh, dear," Rose finally said. "Well, it's not her fault the sheriff locked Mr. James up."

"Should've given him a parade for what he did to Mr. Garrison. That boy deserved a whooping and more!"

Daisy clutched Lily's hand. "Oh, Lily, you don't mean that. Although not everyone's cup of tea, surely Mr. Garrison didn't deserve such a brutal beating."

They all looked back at Trish once again. This time Trish was ready for their stares. She nudged Traitor with her foot until the pup started howling at being disturbed. She bent down to lift him up to her lap, then smiled weakly at her guests.

"Ladies, I believe Miss Cassidy—I mean, Mrs. James—is signaling that she is fed up with our questions." Lily stood up. "Off we go."

Trish and Traitor escorted the Carter sisters to their large blue Cadillac. Lily slid in behind the wheel while Daisy found her spot in the middle of the front seat.

Rose patted Trish's hand. "Now, dearie, tell me. How can we help you get your husband home."

"He'll be home as soon as the sheriff straightens everything out. Dalton was just protecting me."

"And what are you going to be doing, just sitting around here pining for your young man?"

"Oh, no, no!" Trish laughed. She pointed at the fields that were still overrun with weeds. "I've got to figure out a way to get the fields cleaned out. Plus furnish the house. And I still have to take care of the ranch." The smile faded from her face as she realized she was all alone on the ranch for the foreseeable future.

Rose squeezed her hand. "I think we can help with that, Mrs. James."

An hour later, the ranch was buzzing with activity as tractors powered down the lane, followed by trucks piled high with furniture.

Three days later, Trish looked out over the cleared fields, sipping on her morning coffee. The farmers had come and cleared away the downed trees, piling them all in the center of the field, then burned the debris and the field. Finally, they'd installed a solar-powered electric fence encircling the pasture. It was a process that would have taken Dalton and Trish weeks or even months to finish, but with nearly a hundred people turning out to help her, they'd gotten everything done in a few days, clearing the way for the horses to run the extent of their land. The nights she had spent packing up Miranda's things from the master suite and reorganizing all the furniture that had been delivered, a hodge-podge of hand-me-downs, although several of the larger pieces still had store stickers on them.

Dalton would be thrilled with the progress, both inside and out, and she couldn't wait to show it off to him. That had better be sooner than later. She glanced at her watch. The bail hearing in Harrington was still several hours away, so she decided to take the horses out on a run. She and Traitor headed out to the corral, although the dog hung back once she entered the gate. He still had a healthy respect for the horses, but had learned to stay with Trish while staying out of the horses' way. She grabbed Cyrus's reins and led him toward the stable to saddle him, knowing that he would need a strong hand to control him in the newly cleared fields. The Appaloosa would follow wherever Cyrus went.

As they crossed into the stable, Cyrus snorted at her loudly, pulling back sharply on the reins.

"Aren't you the popular one."

Cold spikes of fear stabbed her stomach. He wouldn't dare show his face here, would he?_She glanced up to see a figure leaning against the far door frame. She pulled more tightly on Cyrus's reins to keep him from bolting, although she couldn't blame the horse. She wanted to bolt herself.

"Get off my property before I call the authorities."

Bruce laughed, wincing from the pain, which gave Trish a momentary feeling of satisfaction. She hid her smile, though. His face was no longer swollen, but mottled purple splotches covered almost every inch of skin, and he had a few stitches in his bottom lip and along his cheek.

"Your property? Well, now, miss high and mighty. I didn't realize you had the finances to afford a spread like this." He took several steps, moving closer to her. "Clearly I wasn't charging you enough for rent."

"You're trespassing," she said, gritting her teeth.

He snorted and shook his head, as if talking to a child.

Trish pulled her shoulders back and stood her ground. She refused to let him see her fear. "Do I need to call Sheriff Trudell?"

"My, my, Trish. You grew a spine. Ranch life has changed you."

"Marriage changed me."

Her words stopped Bruce cold, and he glared at her. "Bullshit," he hissed.

Trish shrugged, trying not to enjoy the moment too much. "Call the courthouse. Better yet, ask Sheriff Trudell. He was a witness."

"I don't know what you're playing at—"

"I'm not playing at anything," Trish said, cutting him off. "I'm married, and you're trespassing—and what did I tell you would happen to you if I ever saw you again?"

She stared him down, watching him struggle to control his anger, feeling a sense of satisfaction as he faltered. Coming after her was one thing, but coming after Dalton's wife was something else, and she could see him reliving the pain Dalton had inflicted.

"It's over, Bruce. Accept it and move on."

He frowned and for a second or two she thought maybe he would do something stupid. At that moment, Cyrus reared back on his hind legs and Trish turned to control the stallion, pulling him down and speaking to him calmly. When she turned back, Bruce was gone.

Chapter Nineteen

Dalton sat in the back of Sheriff Trudell's SUV, wishing the man would speed just a little down the country roads. It wasn't like anyone was going to pull him over. Finally, they drove down the lane to the ranch. Dalton could see Trish through the windshield, standing next to Cyrus in the ring. The sheriff had barely opened the back door of the SUV when Dalton pushed past him and stormed up the lane toward Trish, his jaw set and eyes focused only on her.

"You're out?" she asked, but Dalton didn't acknowledge her. "What happened?"

"Mr. Garrison dropped the charges," Sheriff Trudell called out.

"Just like that?"

Dalton grabbed Trish's hand and pulled her after him as he stormed toward Cyrus.

"Dalton, wait!"

But he didn't slow. He grabbed her by the waist and threw her on Cyrus's back, then pulled himself up behind her. Finally, he turned toward the sheriff and Miranda. "Find out who's trespassing on my land, then arrest him." He spun Cyrus around, urged him away from the gate, then urged him on to race across the fields, Traitor trying in vain to keep up.

"Dalton, slow down!" Trish yelled at him, but instead he tightened his arm around her waist. He'd waited three long days and even longer nights to be alone with his wife. He didn't care if the sheriff was offended by his rude behavior. At this moment, Dalton wanted one thing and she was sitting on the horse in front of him.

They topped a hill and, as they moved out of sight of the sheriff and Miranda, Dalton pulled back slightly on the reins. Cyrus seemed all too happy to slow to a comfortable canter, and Trish turned in the saddle to try and speak to Dalton. He took full advantage of her exposed neck, bending down to kiss her tender skin.

His desire had nearly consumed him when he first saw her in the ring, but it was nothing compared to the powerful waves that washed over him when Trish returned his kiss. Cyrus continued his steady pace while Dalton lifted his hand to Trish's left breast, his fingers matching the tempo of his tongue on her neck. She moaned loudly, shifting her hands to rest on his legs, giving him more access to her body. He took full advantage of her offering. He reined in Cyrus, grabbed Trish's waist, lifted her above the saddle, and spun her around to face him, his mouth coming down on hers, demanding and insistent. She matched his passion, giving just as much as he required. She moved her hands down his stomach, reaching down to feel his excitement, causing him to groan even louder as he crushed her against him.

He slid off Cyrus's back, pulling her with him, never breaking their contact. Trish clung to him, as if afraid that he would pull away, but there was nothing on earth that could make him break contact with her. He carried her several feet before setting her down on the soft ground, a cool contrast to the heat emanating from him. He pulled at her clothes, and then he was inside her, thrusting before she had a chance to stop him. Not that she would. She arched into him, calling his name, and he filled her, deeply, completely, carrying her to the edge of the precipice. He matched her rhythm, and they both crescendoed at the same time, finally giving their bodies the relief they had craved for so long.

As she came back to herself, Trish wrapped her arms around Dalton. "Welcome home," she breathed into his ear.

He shifted to look down at her, but remained buried deep inside her. She smiled up at him, and Dalton never felt more content than at this moment. He hugged her to his chest and rolled over until she was looking down at him.

"Well, if this is a welcome home party, I think it's your turn to work, Mrs. James."

Trish pushed back from him, sitting back and straddling him. "With pleasure, Mr. James." She pushed her hips back and forth, slowly building the intensity as Dalton watched her, his eyes thick and smoky with desire. She tossed her head back, then laughed as Dalton rolled once again to be on top of her. "You didn't let me finish," she said.

"Later." His voice was breathless and strained.

"Promise?"

"Yes, anything," he growled at her as his thrusts drove her over the edge once again.

Chapter Twenty

They washed the sweat off each other in the creek, making love once again in the water. Trish was amazed that each time her desire for this man seemed to be even greater than the last, and she wondered how she would ever be able to keep her hands off him. Luckily, she didn't have to figure that out yet.

When her stomach growled, Dalton frowned. "Damn, I guess we have to go back."

She didn't want to go back. She was ready to starve to death if she could do so while his hands and tongue explored her body, but she sighed and agreed that it probably was time.

He put her sideways in the saddle on Cyrus's back before pulling himself up behind her. After turning the horse back toward the house, he dropped his hand to pull her shirt open. "I think I like this position even better than the last one."

She tried to push his hand away, but he just laughed, a deep throaty laugh that turned her insides weak, especially as his fingers brushed lightly against her nipple, hardening it instantly. She pulled one arm around to encircle his waist, then turned to open his shirt, exposing his muscled flesh to her mouth. She explored every inch she could reach, tasting his salty sweat mixed with the cool freshness of the creek. She felt his pulse race and reached up to flick her tongue over the vein pulsating at the base of his neck.

"Trish."

His voice was jagged, and she looked up into his face.

"We'll never get home at this rate."

She smiled up at him. "You want me to stop?"

"No."

"But I probably should?"

"Yes."

"As long as I can finish later."

"Promise?"

"Yes." She smiled and snuggled into his chest, trying to figure out how she had gotten so lucky to have Dalton James fall in love with her. And he did love her, of that she had no doubt. Although he could hide his emotions when he wanted to, he was not hiding them now and his love for her was written across his face. She breathed in deeply, thrilled to know that her love for him was not in vain.

They were heading over the last hill, and soon the ranch would be in full view.

"You didn't even notice all the work I got done on the ranch, did you?"

"I might have, if you weren't so beautiful." He pulled her close, wrapping his arms around her, to kiss her. This kiss was not like the others. It was slow, languid, exploratory, but it made her insides melt just like his others.

The shot rang out, jerking her from her happy thoughts, jerking Dalton away from her. Cyrus reared up, and Dalton struggled to control the horse. Trish realized that having her riding in front was preventing him from having full control over the horse. As if reaffirming her fears, Cyrus reared up again, throwing both Dalton and Trish from his back before bolting away toward the house.

When Trish sat up, her head was spinning, and she fought to gain control of her senses, blinking several times. Traitor was barking in the distance, then his barks were replaced by a whimper. Trish suddenly remembered the sound of the shot before they'd been thrown. "Dalton? Dalton, where are you?"

"He's over here," a woman's voice called out.

Trish whipped around too quickly and felt the corners of her vision blur. She fought the bile rising in the back of her throat and bit down on the inside of her cheek, trying to stay conscious. A red-headed woman stood several feet from her, looking down at a body on the ground, a gun hanging loosely in her hand.

"What did you do?" Trish scrambled to her feet, but her legs wouldn't cooperate. The blackness consumed her before she hit the ground.

Chapter Twenty-One

"Hey, wake up. You okay?"

Trish blinked against the bright afternoon sun, which was making her head explode every time she opened her eyes.

"I think you hit your head."

The voice sounded young. Trish thought she had heard it before, but she couldn't remember for sure.

Dalton! She sat up abruptly, then leaned over to vomit.

"Hey, calm down. You're okay," the voice said.

Trish was finally able to get a good look at the woman. A smattering of freckles was barely visible under her darkened skin. Trish realized that she wasn't a typical redhead with delicate skin. This woman worked outdoors for a living and, given the faded jeans and heavy gloves she wore, could probably ride, rope, and shoot with the best of them. *Shoot!*

"What did you do to him?" Trish glanced around, looking for Dalton.

The woman held up her gloved hands. "It wasn't me. I already called the sheriff to get the guy."

"Dalton? Dalton!"

"He's okay." The woman pointed to an area several yards behind her. "It's just a flesh wound, but looks like he's got quite the goose egg."

Her words catapulted Trish into action. She ignored her shakiness and moved to the still-unconscious Dalton. She noticed a dark bandana tied around his upper arm and realized it was stopping the flow of blood. When she glanced up, the redhead was looking back at her.

"He's gonna be okay," she said.

Trish nodded. "Thank you for helping."

"I don't think the two of us can lift him up on my horse."

Moments later, the sheriff's SUV came over the hill, and the three of them loaded Dalton into the backseat. Trish was relieved when Dalton came to long enough to tell them he was fine and to just let him rest. At the house, they found Miranda waiting for them, having driven over when she found out Dalton had been released. They half carried, half dragged Dalton up the steps and inside, placing him on the sofa in the living room. Trish cleaned out the wound, which turned out to be barely a scratch and hardly worth cleaning.

Meanwhile, Sheriff Trudell interrogated the redhead. "So you didn't shoot Mr. James?"

"No, sheriff—and based on his grumbling when he took off, the man who did wasn't aiming for him."

Trish glanced up at the woman, a sick feeling growing in the pit of her stomach.

"Can you describe what you saw?"

The woman shrugged. "I mostly just saw him from behind. Light, kinda curly hair. Had a shotgun. Clearly wasn't comfortable holding it, and I was about to tell him he was holding the butt of the gun way too high on his shoulder when I saw his target."

Miranda crossed her arms. "Just what were you doing on our property to begin with?"

The woman looked at her feet. Sheriff Trudell almost smiled, but instead cleared his throat. "Mrs. Miranda James, meet Susannah Clark. I believe you know the Clark brothers."

"Yes, I do. They've been driving by my place at all hours of the night, spooking the cattle. Trespassers the lot of them."

Susannah's head jerked up. "Gee, you're welcome. Next time someone's got a gun pulled on your brother, I'll just ride on by."

"Hush, both of you!" Trish said as Sheriff Trudell stepped between the two women. "Miss Clark, I don't know why you were here, but you undoubtedly saved Dalton, so thank you for that." She glanced at Miranda. "Everything else, we'll figure out amicably."

"Now wait a minute," Miranda said.

"No, you're in my house, on my ranch. You'll play by my rules."

"Better listen to her, sis."

They all turned back to the couch, where Dalton was rubbing the back of his head.

"Dalton, are you okay?" Trish knelt in front of him, barely breathing.

He winked at her. "I might need some nursing later on, but for now, I just have one question. When did we get furniture?"

Trish smiled, then stood to hug him tightly.

"Trish, I can't breathe."

"Oh, sorry." She leaned back, but he wrapped his arm around her waist and pulled her to sit next to him.

"So—Susannah, is it?" Dalton looked up at the redhead. "You say you saw him aiming?"

Susannah nodded. "Yeah, but I startled him, so the shot didn't hit his target. He whipped around so fast, caught me off guard. He slapped me down and when I looked up, you, sir, were on the ground next to me."

Sheriff Trudell looked at Susannah's face. "Slapped you down? Are you okay?"

"Nothing I can't handle," she said, waving him off. She glanced at the others. "Four older brothers."

Trish chewed on her bottom lip. She'd known the minute Susannah had described the assailant that it was Bruce. Now he was coming after Dalton, and she didn't think he'd react well to that news.

Dalton had apparently come to the same conclusion. "So he drops the charges so he can come after me personally."

Sheriff Trudell nodded. "Seems so."

"Don't just stand there, sheriff." Miranda's hands-on-hips posture was commanding, but her voice had lost some of its shrillness.

"I think you missed some key information," Susannah said. "He wasn't aiming for Mr. James there."

They all looked at Trish. When she looked at Dalton, she could see the fury taking control.

"Son of a bitch!" he hissed, launching himself off the couch. "Sheriff, you'd better find him before I do."

"You are not going after him, Dalton."

Again, all eyes turned to Trish, but she was only concerned about the dark caramel eyes burning into her.

"Don't tell me what to do, woman." His voice was a growl, and he stared her down for a moment before turning toward the door.

"Dalton James!" Trish stood up and grabbed his arm, spinning him around to face her.

The sheriff cleared his throat and motioned to the other two women. "Why don't we step out on the porch?"

"And miss all the fun?" Miranda smiled until Dalton glanced at her with his glowering stare. "Fine—but speak up so we can hear everything."

"That won't be a problem." Dalton spoke through gritted teeth as everyone filed past him, closing the door to leave him and Trish alone.

Trish didn't wait for him to start the fight. "Don't you dare leave me, especially not to go after that slime. I finally get my husband back and you want to run off again?"

"He shot me on my land."

"Our land!" She put her hand on his chest and looked up into his eyes, speaking quietly now. "So do you think leaving me now is smart? Let the sheriff handle it."

Dalton's chest heaved, and she could tell he was still fuming. He ran his hand through his hair in frustration.

"Stay, Dalton. Protect me." It was almost a whisper, but it gave him pause as he considered the ramifications. She pressed her advantage. "I'll do whatever you tell me."

"Ha!"

"I promise, Dalton. Whatever you tell me."

Dalton glared down at her, but she could see the heat of his anger being replaced by a different kind of heat. He spun around and headed to front door, sticking his head out. "Sheriff, find him, arrest him, press every damn charge you can find against him." He slammed the door and turned the deadbolt, locking it loudly before returning to Trish.

"Thank you, Dalton."

"Don't thank me yet." He swept her up in his arms and carried her to the stairs. "Did you get bedroom furniture too?"

Epilogue

Trish stood on the porch, resting her grocery bag on the railing as she watched Dalton work the horse in the ring. He was shirtless, and she enjoyed seeing his muscles rippling even from this distance. She knew she should go inside before her stares got her in trouble. They'd been married almost a year, but still one look from her could cause Dalton to forget what he was doing and carry her away to some secluded place for an afternoon of love-making.

It was a power she was all too happy to wield over him.

"Afternoon, ma'am."

Trish looked down to see Susannah at the foot of the steps. "Susannah, how many times have I told you—"

"I know, I know." Susannah laughed. "But you've just done wonders for Lucas."

Trish and Susannah both looked to the ring, where a tall muscular man with several inches on Dalton was trading places with him to work the next horse.

"Your brother has done wonders for this ranch, Susannah."

Both women knew that Promise Ranch had grown tremendously in the past few months after word got out that its top trainer could work with any horse, no matter how challenging. Lucas had a hard time dealing with people, especially after losing his wife while he was fighting in the war in Afghanistan, but horses were a different story. Since he started working at Promise Ranch, he'd become one of the most respected men in the ranching community. Trish smiled to herself. She thought Miranda had something to do with Lucas coming out of his shell, but she'd keep that tidbit to herself. For now, at least.

"Well, I just stopped by to see how he was doing." Susannah nodded again, then headed for her truck.

"Make sure you tell the sheriff hello for me," Trish called out after her, giggling when she saw Susannah blush as she ducked into her truck. She waved at the young woman as she drove out of the lane.

"So you planning on working today?"

Trish glanced over at Dalton, who was walking toward the porch. She held up the grocery bag. "Feeding you is work."

He licked his lips and sauntered closer to her, keeping the railing between them. "You don't need food to feed me, sweetheart."

She set the bag down and placed her hands on the railing, leaning over it. She was playing with fire and she knew it, but today was a day to celebrate. "I stopped at the courthouse."

Dalton's face clouded over, and his jaw went tight.

"Calm down, Dalton. The verdict came in."

"And?"

"Let's just say we won't have to worry about him until our kids are in college."

"It's still too soon, if you ask me." Dalton crossed his arms and frowned.

Trish watched him, waiting for the change that she knew would come. She was not disappointed.

"But kids, huh?" He smiled again, leaning up to kiss her lightly. "When are we going to get started on those kids, anyway?"

"Well, Mr. James, apparently you already have."

She watched his face as understanding spread over it, followed by the biggest smile she'd ever seen from him. At that moment, her love for this man swelled even more, and Trish was afraid her heart would burst from her chest.

Dalton hoisted himself over the railing and pulled her close. "Are you sure?"

"The doc seemed pretty darn sure you'd done something right."

Dalton whooped so loudly he scared the horses. Lucas called out to make sure everything was okay.

"Everything's great, Lucas! You're in charge for the day." Dalton looked down at Trish and said, "We've got some celebrating to do, Mrs. James. And baby."

"And babies," she corrected. "Twins."

Dalton whooped again, then swept Trish up in his arms and carried her inside. "I love you, Trish, and I promise I always will."

"I love you too, Dalton, and I promise I always will." It was a promise that she looked forward to keeping.

Acknowledgments

Life in a small town is often depicted as having a Mayberryesque quality, and in many areas, this picture holds true. Yet small towns also tend to be quite challenging, especially for anyone who steps outside the boundaries of "the way things have always been done."

I was one of those who could never follow the norm. Still can't, in fact. Luckily, I have been able to find friends who accept me, support me, challenge me to push further, and still answer my 2 a.m. phone calls, knowing full well that I will likely ramble on for hours and hours about nothing in particular while still somehow coming up with solutions to the world's most pressing problems (okay, maybe not the world's problems…).

For all of you who have endured my never-ending musings, I truly am grateful that you continue to answer the phone.

Turn the page for a sneak peek at

Heart So Sweet

Book 3 in the Great Plains Romance series

Susannah Clark sat fuming in the back of the sheriff's SUV. In all her twenty-two years she'd never been inside a police car, never had any of her own legal issues, and now she was being escorted home by the new sheriff after witnessing the attempted murder of Dalton James and his new bride, Trish. Susannah had tried to stop Trish's ex from firing on the couple as they rode back to their ranch house and, luckily, Dalton had only been grazed by the bullet, but she knew she wouldn't get out of this situation unscathed. Sooner or later the questions would start, and something about this lawman told her he wouldn't just let it go.

"You okay back there?" His deep voice startled her, making her heart jump.

"I'll be better when you let me out of this car."

He turned away, muffling a noise that Susannah recognized. He was laughing at her!

Although his mirrored sunglasses hid a large swath of his face, she could see an aquiline nose that fit his strong jawline well. He wore his hair a little longer than she expected of a sheriff, almost as if he was overdue for a visit to the barber, and his black hair already showed a few streaks of gray, although Susannah would be surprised if he was even in his thirties. There was just something about him....

"I don't understand why I have to ride back here anyway. It's not like I did anything wrong. Hell, I saved two people today!"

"Department policy."

Susannah looked at him via the rear view mirror and blinked. "Excuse me?"

"No passengers up front. Department policy."

She rolled her eyes, wishing she could see behind his mirrored sunglasses. She had a feeling that he was still laughing at her, which gave her the sudden urge to rip off his sunglasses and crush them in her hands.

She frowned and looked out her window. She needed to stop wasting time on the sheriff and figure out how she was going to get herself and her family out of the mess her brothers created. Susannah scowled in frustration. Her older brothers Andrew, Daniel, and Jonathan were always getting in trouble, always costing the family bail money, although Andrew was the real troublemaker. Daniel just wanted to ride his coattails while Jonathan got dragged along. Only Lucas, the oldest, stayed out of trouble, but he had his own issues, far worse than what the others were dealing with.

"Most innocent people don't get so jumpy sitting in the backseat."

Susannah's brows furrowed together, and she pursed her lips into a light white line. He was goading her, and she knew it. She crossed her arms and made a show of turning away from him to look out the window once again. His quiet chuckle made every muscle in her body scream in fury, but she would not give him the satisfaction of seeing her react. She curled her toes tightly in her boots, concentrating all her anger there. It was a trick she learned while growing up with her brothers, a way to express her anger without them seeing. If they knew they were getting to her, it was like adding gasoline to an open flame.

She needed to keep her anger hidden. For now. But once they got back to her farm, she'd let loose, knowing that her brothers would quickly rally around her. For all their trouble-making, they were extremely loyal. And they damn sure better be there today after she saved their butts.

Susannah sighed. She didn't think this sheriff would care about who did what or why. Old Sheriff Enger would've come out to the farm to lecture the boys and, because he'd been a close friend of their father's, the boys would listen. For a bit. Things would calm down for a while, and everyone would breathe easier. This new sheriff couldn't be much older than her brothers. They certainly would not take to him one bit. Susannah sighed again, realizing what she would be in for: cleaning up more of her brothers' antics.

A little of the sting of her anger dissipated when she realized that the sheriff was driving her right to the one place he shouldn't be going. Her brothers would likely be there, still smarting from the scolding she'd given them when she found them cutting the fence along Dalton James' property line—the line he shared with their grazing land. Not only that, but they were stealing tools from Dalton, all to get back at his sister, Miranda, who the boys swore was stealing the family's cattle. When she'd first learned what they were doing, Susannah had lashed out at them like their momma used to do when they were younger. She had scared them with that tirade. Truth be told, she had scared herself a bit too. But apparently it hadn't been enough, because this afternoon she'd had to ride out to the Jameses' horse ranch and confront her brothers, who were back at their shenanigans. When her anger boiled over, it had surpassed anything they'd ever seen in their momma, and the boys had high-tailed it back to the farm, leaving Susannah to walk the fence line and try to fix the damage.

That was when she'd seen Bruce Garrison taking aim at the two riders on a horse.

Susannah was glad she intervened, saving both Dalton and Trish. But she hadn't realized the predicament it would put her in, having to explain her presence on their property. Questions would inevitably arise and here she was, leading the sheriff right to the lair of the vandals—vandals who would more than likely brag about their efforts, seeing that they perceived themselves to be the victims. After all, Miranda James was stealing their cattle. Well, that's what Andrew said. Susannah wasn't convinced. She sighed loudly again. Andrew had done it again, created a total mess for the family—namely, her—to clean up.

"You okay, Miss Clark? Maybe need to get something off your chest?"

Susannah rolled her eyes, then winced at the bruise on the side of her face where Bruce had struck her down before running away. She could feel her anger rising again, furious at Andrew for risking the entire farm, the only thing they had left of their parents. But Andrew wasn't here, so she'd just have to take her anger out on the sheriff. "Actually, I do."

She saw him frown in the rear view mirror, then he slowed the SUV and pulled to stop along the shoulder. He turned around in his seat to look at her, finally taking off his sunglasses. "Are you sure, Annie?"

His voice was quiet, and Susannah almost didn't hear his words, but not because of the steely reserve that kept his voice low. It was his eyes that shocked her into silence. Rich, cobalt blue eyes stared at her, taking her breath away. She'd only seen one person who had eyes that shade of blue, but he had left

Harrington County nearly a decade ago, when she was just a little girl with a giant crush. It couldn't be him...could it?

She studied his features more closely, his strong jawline coming to a rounded chin under lips that were perfectly proportioned to his face. His skin, which she'd originally taken for tanned, was actually more of an olive complexion. A lock of hair fell across his forehead, and he pushed it back in a way that was familiar to her. And he had called her Annie. Only two people in the world called her that: her brother Lucas and his best friend.

"Tate?"

She wasn't sure she said it out loud, that it wasn't just an echo in her mind, but his large expressive eyes registered something new...amusement?

Susannah frowned. "Tate Trudell, what the hell are you doing back here?"

The corner of his mouth lifted in a half-smile, showing a dimple on his left cheek. Oh, how Susannah had dreamed about that dimple when she was younger, and now here it was, back in her life again. She felt her stomach flip-flop, and she told herself that it was just because she was worried about how she would convince him that she just happened to be in the right place at the right time earlier today. Tate would know immediately that her brothers were involved—hell, he'd probably already figured it out. She tried to maintain a pleasant smile while groaning inwardly. He knew her brothers almost as well as she did, probably even better in some ways.

"Sit tight, Annie." His voice had returned to its authoritarian manner, and Tate shifted to step outside the car.

Susannah watched him walk along the side of the car, his right hand resting on his gun in its holster. She twisted around to see Bruce Garrison, the man who shot at Dalton James, about thirty yards behind the SUV, jogging toward the trees along the opposite side of the road. Tate called out to him, and Bruce stopped in the middle of the road, facing Tate, the rifle he'd used on Dalton still in his hand. Tate stood by the back bumper of the SUV, his hand still on his gun. Why hadn't he drawn?

"Tate! That's him! Tate?"

He made no indication that he had heard her, and Susannah whipped around to try to open her door, but she knew it was futile. Even the window wouldn't roll down.

She turned back to knock on the driver-side window, but as she did, she heard the crack of gunfire. Her heart jumped to her throat. She saw Bruce fall to the ground, and she breathed a sigh of relief. Until she realized Tate was no longer standing next to the SUV. She pulled herself to the driver's side seat and pressed her face to the window.

Tate was face down on the ground, and he wasn't moving.

Susannah pounded on the window. Tate remained sprawled on his stomach along the side of the SUV.

This was all a dream, it had to be a dream—or a nightmare—but it couldn't be real. "Tate, oh my God, Tate, please be okay."

She pulled on the door handle, but of course it wouldn't open. She was still in the back of a police car, after all. And there were no handles to roll down the windows. She leaned back and kicked at the windows with the heel of her cowboy boots, but the glass wouldn't break.

Susannah growled in frustration, then looked around to see if she could find anything in the car to call for help. She had rushed out of the house that afternoon without her cell phone, but she saw Tate's sitting on the front seat next to the console with the police radio. She pushed on the steel cage separating the front seat from the back, but it wouldn't give. She tried to squeeze her fingers through the holes in the cage, but unless they grew about six inches longer, they would never be able to reach anything on the other side.

She examined every part of the cage, especially where it met with the roof of the SUV. Pulling on the edging, trying to pry it loose, made no difference. The cage just wouldn't budge. She swore loudly, using a phrase that would make even her brothers blush. Then she screamed loudly in frustration.

"Tate Trudell, when I get out of here, I am going to kill you for putting me in the backseat!"

Her stomach lurched as she realized he might already be dead.

Books in the Great Plains Romance Series

Vibrant Heart

When the ever-organized Melanie Olson returns to her small Nebraska hometown to prove to the commitment-phobe Raymond what a mistake he made, a flat tire threatens to ruin all her plans. Luckily, cowboy-turned-entrepreneur Jake Monroe stops to help the woman stranded by the side of the road, unaware that his world is about to be turned on end. Realizing that she's traveling to the same wedding he is, he decides fate has dealt him a winning hand—until he discovers that she only has eyes for the town womanizer. Jake is determined to get the beautiful spitfire to look his way, but her intensity might be too much for even him to handle.

A Heart's Promise

Trish Cassidy is an easygoing woman with a goal: to manage her own ranch. But after her parents' death, she finds herself stuck with a dominating boyfriend who has probably just ruined her last chance to connect with the local ranchers. Just when she thinks she must give up on her dream, the enigmatic Dalton James steps into her life, offering an opportunity to build a ranch from the ground up. What she doesn't expect is her powerful attraction to her new boss—or how controlling he starts to become.

When Dalton James decided to build his horse ranch, the last thing he anticipated was saving a damsel in distress. Then again, Trish Cassidy isn't someone who needs saving. So why is he so protective of her? More importantly, why does he feel like he has to do the right thing around her, even when she doesn't want him to?

Heart So Sweet

With four older brothers, rancher Susannah Clark is used to dealing with men and getting them out of trouble. But when her childhood crush Tate Trudell returns as sheriff of Harrington County, Susannah must decide whether to save her brothers yet again, even if means losing the man she loves.

Tate Trudell never expected to move back to Harrington, especially after how he left things with his best friend, Lucas Clark, just before Lucas left for the war in Afghanistan. But a lot has changed in ten years, including Susannah, Lucas' little sister. When Tate discovers that her passion matches his own, he's determined to be with her. To get the woman of his dreams, he must work through his bad blood with the Clark family—if Lucas doesn't kill him first.

So Wills the Heart

When the tough gets going, artist Evie Jacobson runs away. So when her great aunt leaves her a property in rural Nebraska, Evie uses the opportunity to escape her boss, who's deluded himself into thinking she loves him. But life in the country is a bit too tame for Evie—until she meets Jonathan Clark, a man who tests the limits of her spontaneity. When Evie discovers that Jonathan might not be everything she expected, will she runaway yet again or will she have the strength to stay and face her greatest test?

Jonathan Clark's afternoon break from working the ranch turns into a fantasy-come-to-life when he encounters Evie Jacobson skinny dipping in a private pond. His water nymph's playful side excites him like no woman he's ever met, and he looks for any excuse to be with her. But a rancher's work is never done, and Jonathan must choose between his family and Evie—a woman who might have already moved on to someone else.

My Heart, My Gift

Can the big city girl convince the small-town cowboy to give Christmas a second chance? Or will the secret she hides destroy any chance of a relationship between them?

When Serafina Anderson makes a mess of her first semester of college, she does what she knows best: avoids facing her parents. This time she runs away to spend her winter vacation at the ranch of her cousin, Trish. Her escapades also lead her right into the arms of Andrew Clark, the small town's most notorious troublemaker. But Sera sees beyond Andrew's crass nature and recognizes that the bad boy isn't as bad as everyone makes him out to be.

Andrew Clark hates Christmas—at least he has since his parents died. He refuses to buy into the commercialism of the holiday and does his best to shove the hurt he feels down so deep inside him that no one will ever find it. So when Sera ignores his bad temper and rude remarks, he wonders if he's finally found the angel who can rescue him from himself—until he discovers that she's been lying to him all along.

About the Author

Corrissa James was not always a country girl. In fact, she fought it all her life, traveling the world to live in far-flung cities like St. Petersburg, Russia, Caracas, Venezuela, Varanasi, India, and Guadalajara, Mexico. She didn't realize she was meant to live in the country until she returned to her roots in Nebraska, where she discovered the beauty of the fields around her (even if she was allergic to them) and the intensity of Mother Nature (who sure packs a wallop!).

Corrissa wrote her first romance stories in junior high, although at the time she didn't really know what happened after kissing, so she improvised with lots of ellipses (…). Her professional writing career initially took her away from romance—but never far away as Corrissa could always be found with a romance book at hand.

Today she focuses on western romance novellas, offering afternoon reads focused on strong women and the men they choose (never without some struggles along the way).

If you've enjoyed this book, please leave a review.

Thank you!

Check out more works by Corrissa James and see
what's coming next by visiting
www.corrissajames.com

www.ingramcontent.com/pod-product-compliance
Lightning Source LLC
Chambersburg PA
CBHW061210170626
46809CB00003B/1306